Helen Humphreys is a novelist an[...] the UK, and now lives in Kingston, [...] novel, *Leaving Earth*, was a *New York Times* Notable Book in 1998 and won the City of Toronto Book Award. Her other novels include *Afterimage*, *The Lost Garden*, and *Coventry*.

"In order to ventriloquize a long-forgotten, peculiar Frenchman, Humphreys has added to her trademark exquisite prose a stylish wryness. Witty, sad and gorgeous in equal measure, this story of a man like no other probes love like a wound" Emma Donoghue

"A real exploration of the heart. Strange and amusing at times, this tender, life-affirming novel made me contemplate love in a whole new way" Amanda Smyth

"Humphreys' pacing and story-telling are well-honed... an engaging novel told with wit and imagination" Nathan Brooker, *Financial Times*

"Seductive... love is finally reinvented, restored to its purity, in this haunting, moving and stylish study of hearts laid bare. Set against a vividly evoked picture of a generation in love with love, it is a compelling exploration of desire and its tentacular costs" David Coward, *TLS*

"Humphreys treats her curious, fascinating material with deft wit and restraint" *New Books*

"This is an illuminating and unique portrait of a strange and beautiful love between two flawed characters. The wry and witty tone with which the story is delivered contributes greatly to the intrigue and fascination" *Sunday Herald Sun*, Australia

"Beautifully paced, elegantly written and compelling from start to fin[...]

THE REINVENTION OF LOVE

Helen Humphreys

A complete catalogue record for this book can be obtained from the
British Library on request

The right of Helen Humphreys to be identified as the author of this work has been
asserted by her in accordance with the Copyright, Designs and Patents Act 1988

Copyright © 2011 Helen Humphreys

First published in Canada in 2011 by HarperCollins Publishers Ltd

First published in the UK in this paperback edition in 2012 by Serpent's Tail
First published in the UK in 2011 by Serpent's Tail,
an imprint of Profile Books Ltd
3A Exmouth House
Pine Street
London EC1R 0JH
website: www.serpentstail.com

ISBN: 978 1 84668 799 0
eISBN: 978 1 84765 760 2

Designed and typeset by sue@lambledesign.demon.co.uk

Printed and bound in Great Britain by
CPI Group (UK) Ltd, Croydon, CR0 4YY

10 9 8 7 6 5 4 3 2 1

In memory of my brother, Martin

"Le vrai, le vrai seul"

Sainte-Beuve

PARIS, 1830s

CHARLES

IT SEEMS I AM TO DIE AGAIN.

He slapped my face. I called him a "glorious inferior". (Not in that order.) And here we are, in this rainy wood in the middle of the working week, trying to kill each other.

Let me explain.

I want to tell you everything.

The board meeting was long and dreary. I was tired. When the senior editor asked me to shorten my article, I objected. I am only a junior writer at the newspaper, but I am much more intelligent than anyone else there, and sometimes I just can't pretend otherwise. It was careless of me to insult Monsieur Dubois because I know the possible consequences of such an action. And I was not disappointed. He practically sprang across the table to strike my face. His challenge could be heard by people walking outside on the crowded boulevard.

Antoine is my reluctant second. He is out of the cab already, the wooden case with the duelling pistols tucked securely under one arm. "Come on," he says. "They're waiting." And, through the open door of the cab I can see Pierre Dubois and his second, the print runner, Bernard, standing under a straggly stand of trees at the edge of the wood.

"I haven't even had my breakfast," I say, struggling to open my umbrella before I step down onto the soggy ground.

"Get out," says Antoine, unsympathetically, and I feel like challenging *him* to a duel for his insolence. I snap open my umbrella.

"Please be serious," he says.

"What?"

"That." He gestures towards the green umbrella with the yellow handle. I had thought it very dashing when I purchased it from a Paris shop last week. But I can see that here, out in nature, it looks a bit ridiculous.

"Lower it," he says.

"I will not. I don't mind being killed, but I refuse to get wet."

We march off moodily into the wood.

Pierre Dubois also appears disheartened by my umbrella. It seems to make him feel sad for me, and perhaps he has second thoughts about shooting such a pitiful creature.

"You can offer me a profound apology," he says, "and we can forget all about this."

We are writers. We are meant to brandish pens, not pistols. I regret my insult. Pierre obviously regrets his challenge. I could apologize and we could share a cab back to the city and resume the business of making a newspaper.

But words are not easy to set aside. They make a shape in the mouth, a shape in the air. When something is said, it exists, and it is not easily persuaded again into silence. The truth is that I *do* think Pierre Dubois is my inferior. The truth is that I annoy him beyond reason and he would like to fire me, but he can't because the readers are so fond of my reviews.

"I take nothing back," I say.

"You are a fool," says Pierre.

"You are a bigger fool."

Now we can't wait to shoot each other. Antoine opens the case and loads the pistols. Bernard has disappeared behind a tree to relieve himself.

The gun is heavy and smells of scorch and earth. I clutch it to my breast and pace off into the trees, counting the twenty strides under my breath, pausing only once when my umbrella snags in the branches overhead.

Pierre has challenged me, so I am to shoot first. I stop. I turn. I raise my hand with the pistol in it and sight down my arm. Pierre is partially obscured by scrub. The rain erases his outline. I squint, then I pull the trigger. The gun kicks and smokes, and for a moment I can't see anything. Someone yells and I'm afraid I have hit Pierre, but when the smoke clears he remains as he was, standing in the rain in the middle of some bushes.

Now it is Pierre's turn.

The bright green umbrella will help guide the lead ball to its target, but I refuse to sheath it because I had insisted on bringing it. But what if my stubbornness causes my death? It occurs to me, for the first time, that I am perhaps too wilful for my own good, that I am not helped by my character, that it potentially causes me great harm, and that I should probably fight hard against it.

"You will get another shot," says Antoine, appearing suddenly at my side. "Give me the pistol and I'll reload for you."

I pass it to him, and turn so that I can present the full fleshly target of my body to Pierre Dubois.

It is then that I think of Adèle, and how, if I die, she will weep and despair and be impressed by my courage. So, I had better summon some courage. I take a deep breath and hold it, close my eyes, and brace myself for the sting and the first bitter taste of darkness.

HE IS MY NEIGHBOUR. We live two doors apart on Notre-Dame-des-Champs. He is also my dear friend. I am also in love with his wife.

Of Victor's poetry I can say that nothing is better. Of his plays, nothing is worse. It is prudent of him, perhaps, to have recently become a novelist. But whatever he does he is wildly successful, driven by an appetite for glory that I envy and admire. I like to think that my glowing reviews of his poetry have helped to make him so famous. Certainly our friendship has blossomed because of my praise. It has also inspired my own writing and I have dedicated the first volume of my poems to Victor. Friendship is a consolation to me. I believe in its properties as some believe in religion.

But it doesn't seem to have helped my book sales.

Have I mentioned already that I am in love with Victor's wife, Adèle? To say that this complicates the friendship for me is an understatement. But for Victor, who knows nothing of my passion for Adèle, our friendship remains joyful and uncomplicated.

The Hugos have four children, the last, little Adèle, my goddaughter, was born just a few months ago. Their house is noisy and crowded, alive with laughter and schemes. I delight in its tumult after the calm seas of my own empty domicile.

Tonight, after my rather invigorating day in the countryside duelling with Monsieur Dubois, I enter to find Victor and Adèle in the kitchen with two men. There is a jug of wine on the table. The men are drinking and pacing. Adèle sits in a chair with a large sheet of paper spread out on her lap. Several of the children run through the kitchen at intervals, chasing each other with a butterfly net and shrieking like birds at the zoo.

I am so often at the Hugos' house that it has long ceased to be necessary for me to knock at the door and wait to be admitted. I just walk in.

"Charles," says Victor, when he sees me standing in the kitchen doorway. "We are plotting. Come and help us." He claps me on the back and passes his own glass of wine to me. "I think you know Theo and Luc."

The young men who hang on the genius of Victor Hugo look indistinguishable to me. Theo could be Luc could be Henri could be Pascal. They are interchangeable, these admirers, and the great poet treats them with benevolence, but he uses them like servants.

I nod at the men, who glance my way briefly and then return their rapt attention to Victor.

"Here," says Adèle, patting the chair beside hers. "Come and join me." She looks up with her beautiful brown eyes and just the suggestion of a smile on her lips. I sit down. Our heads are a whisper apart. She has her hair up tonight. Often she does this so hastily that the twists of dark hair look like a nest of glossy sausages sitting atop of her perfectly shaped head.

"What are you doing?"

"Marching into battle," says Victor, fetching a fresh glass and pouring himself some more wine. "Slaying the enemy."

I look at the piece of paper on Adèle's lap. It's a seating map for the Comédie-Française.

"The anti-romantics don't like *Hernani*," she explains. "There are hecklers every night."

"Ignorants," shouts Victor. The children screech through the kitchen, waving the butterfly net like a gauzy flag.

Hernani is the latest of Victor's wretched plays. This time, the melodrama is about two lovers who poison each other. The irony is not lost on me.

"We're planting supporters. Here." Adèle moves a finger across the drawing of the theatre balcony. "And here." She moves her finger down to the dress circle and her arm gently grazes mine. I feel her touch all through my body. The jolt is as sharp as being shot.

"Everyone you can think of must be persuaded to come," says Victor. "We must outnumber the enemy."

"Is it the same hecklers every night then?" I ask.

"We think so." Adèle pulls the seating diagram across her lap so that she can move her leg and press it against mine.

I can't breathe. I am starting to perspire. The glass of wine trembles in my hand.

"Charles?" says Victor. He looks over at me and I jerk my knee away from Adèle's. The seating diagram jumps with the sudden movement.

"What?"

"Would you take my wife?"

"What?" My voice squeaks. I spill some wine on my shoe.

"To the theatre," says Adèle, evenly. "He means, would you take me to the theatre?"

But the look that Victor gives me is a shrewd one. I know the man well enough to sense that he suspects something. We have not been as careful as we thought. The arrogance that snares all lovers has caught us up. He is testing me with his question.

"I'd be honoured," I say, with as much aplomb as I can muster. But he is not fooled. He turns away, and he is not fooled.

We manage a moment in the upstairs hallway after Adèle has put the children to bed.

I put my hands in her hair. She buries her face in my neck.

"I love your perfume," she says.

"I love you," I say.

Downstairs I hear Victor bellow like a cow being slaughtered. He can be so loud, so coarse. I slide my hands down to Adèle's breasts and give them a squeeze. She backs up against the wall and we press our bodies together.

"Leave him," I whisper. "Come away with me. I can't bear that we aren't together."

Adèle looks confused. We are, in fact, only a fraction of an inch apart.

"That we aren't always together," I say.

This is our sticking point. Even from his vile plays, Victor makes money. The Hugos are rich. Adèle has four children. I am a penniless critic, an unsuccessful poet.

But the depth of love that I offer Adèle is considerable, and so we sway together in the upstairs hallway of my best friend's house, until little Adèle calls out in her sleep and the balance shifts away from me and back towards her family.

"Tomorrow," she says. "We will walk out tomorrow. I will leave the children with my sister." She kisses me, urgent and sweet, and then goes in to calm her youngest daughter.

Victor is still in the kitchen when I go downstairs. Theo and Luc have disappeared.

"Charles," he says. "Come and sit with me."

I do as he says, declining his offer of another glass of wine.

The house is quiet now. I can hear the chatter of insects through the open window. A breeze carries the scent of roses into the room. I suddenly feel overwhelmed with hopelessness. Adèle will never leave her family. She will tire of me. I will always be lonely and alone.

"I heard you were in a duel this morning," says Victor.

"Yes." I wish I had thought to mention this to Adèle.

"Did you challenge?"

"No. It was a trifling matter," I say. "An ongoing quarrel between me and the senior editor at the *Globe*."

"Ah." Victor spreads out his hands on the table, already bored by my troubles. "What do you think of *Hernani*?" The people who oppose his romantic play are getting under his skin, despite his noisy bravado.

"I have only seen it in rehearsal," I say, honestly. "And a play can't be properly judged from a rehearsal. The actors are always holding back."

"Will you go this week?" asks Victor. "Will you tell me truly what you think of it?"

"I will."

Victor clasps me to him as fiercely and as passionately as I had clasped Adèle to me in the upstairs hallway.

"You are such a friend to me, Charles," he says. "I don't know what I'd do without you."

Adèle surprises me at the gate. She is wearing white and looks ghostly among the dark trunks of the plane trees.

Every moment that I am in her company is glorious. I forget my despair in the kitchen. We love each other. It will end happily. How could it be otherwise?

"My darling," she says, "Victor told me that you were in a duel. Were you nearly killed?" She is all shivery with the danger of it.

"The first shot grazed my temple," I say, "and the second burned off the buttons on my waistcoat." The lie is delicious and we both savour it for a full moment.

In fact, both of Pierre's shots were wildly off their mark. One of my shots hit a tree. The other couldn't even be found. Bernard had brought bread and cheese and jam, and when the rain stopped we all had a picnic under the trees before returning to the office.

"You must not die," says Adèle. "I couldn't live without you."

"I won't die," I say, and I mean it.

She kisses me, a different kiss from the one she gave me in the house. This one has a note of desperation to it. This is the kiss for a lover who has almost met his mortal end. It has a mixture of surrender and commitment that I find intoxicating. The insects offer their applause. It strikes me that this is what I have always wanted, from myself, and from another. I want to give myself entirely. I want to pledge myself completely. I want a moment such as this one, a moment from which I might never fully recover.

IT IS MY FIRST SIGNIFICANT MEMORY, a memory I have carried into adulthood, undisturbed and unquestioned. There is, in this memory, much of what I am experiencing now, as I look back on my life.

First, let me tell you about my beginnings, some sixty years ago.

I was born at 9 a.m. on December 23, 1804, at Boulogne-sur-Mer. My parents were old when they married – my father fifty-one, my mother over forty. I was their only child. In fact, my father died of the quinsy just before I was born. My cradle rested on a coffin.

My father was an official in the Customs and Excise department, but he had an interest in literature. I have his small library of books, most of them annotated heavily in the margins, as though he were deep in conversation with the authors. He was particularly fond of Virgil.

My mother was the daughter of mariners. I remember she used to sing me sea shanties to lull me into sleep.

I am my father – Charles. I am my mother – Augustin(e). But my mother never called me anything but my surname: Sainte-Beuve.

We lived quietly in Boulogne, my mother and I, in the lower town, mere steps from the busy harbour where my father used to work. When I was eighteen I left for Paris to attend medical school, and I took Mother with me. I have rarely returned to the town of my birth. The sea does not interest me, or haunt me. It is too vast. It is unknowable.

But this is not a memory of where I first lived. This is a memory of how, when I was six years old, I was taken to see the first Napoleon – Napoleon Bonaparte. My mother had dressed me in a little hussar uniform and I was walked up the hill that overlooked the town, to watch the great general review his troops.

He was a slight man, such as I used to be, but at the time he seemed magnificent and huge. I remember the flutter of his hands and the white mask of his face, the shiny gold buttons on his uniform, the silence of the soldiers as he paraded up and down in front of them. At one moment I was close enough to reach out and touch his coat-tails, but I did not dare.

I was raised by my elderly mother and her equally elderly sister. My nickname as a boy at school was "Pussy". I lived in a house of women. Perhaps this is why I was so impressed by Napoleon. He was a powerful man in charge of other men. He was what I imagined a father might be.

Four years later, when he met his defeat by the British at Waterloo, I cried myself to sleep in the cold darkness of my bedroom.

So this is what comes back to me all these years later – the brightness of the day on the hill, the excitement of being so near to greatness and glory, to a famous man I could reach out and touch if I wanted to; and then the tears and loneliness, the scratchy wool blanket on my cheek as I lay face down on my bed and sobbed for the man who had left me again.

There is something of Napoleon in Victor. The way he strutted up and down in his kitchen the night he had the seating plan for the Comédie-Française, reviewing his troops, planning his battle for control of the theatre.

Exultation and at the same time despair. That is what I felt with regard to Napoleon, what I have continued to feel all my life with regard to everything else.

There are so many memories from childhood. Why does one

stand out above all others? Perhaps because a few events are not particular to childhood, even though they occur there. Perhaps some memories are more a foretelling than the reminder of an event that belongs entirely in the past. Perhaps what we remember is merely a continuing truth about ourselves.

The story tastes of the man.

WHO SEES LOVE ARRIVING? Who can gauge the movements one person makes towards another? Movements so slight, so tentative, that they are almost invisible.

It is impossible to watch love arriving, but it is abundantly clear when it has arrived.

I remember the moment perfectly.

At first, when I visited the Hugos, I would make sure to go in the evening, when I knew that Victor would be home. In the early days, after I had reviewed his poems so favourably, after I had called him, in print, "a genius", he had plenty of time for me. I would go to his house after supper and we would talk together long into the evening, about poetry and literature, about the passion we both felt for writing. Adèle was sometimes in the room, sitting sewing by the fire, often silent. Victor is prone to long monologues when he gets excited and though she would sometimes try to say a few words, to join our discussion, he would talk right over her.

He would do this with the children too, swat them away if he was busy proclaiming – but he would also, if he wasn't occupied, bend down with them to examine an ant in the grass. It was then that I envied him, when he casually laid a hand on his son's head, or looked with real interest at the drawing his daughter had brought to him. But he was cavalier with his family. He failed to recognize the gift they were and appreciated them only when it suited him.

One day I walked round after lunch to return a book I

had borrowed and I found Adèle alone with her young ones. She invited me to stay and I sat with her by the pond in the garden while the children buzzed around us. Without Victor's presence, Adèle was more talkative, and I remember we had a very pleasant discussion about poetry. She invited me to come again, and so I started to visit in the afternoons when I knew Victor would be out, as well as in the evenings, when I knew Victor would be in.

Adèle and I sat in the drawing room, reading to each other, or walked out with the children to the Jardin du Luxembourg, which was mere minutes away from her house. These were very pleasant excursions and I was content to cultivate my friendship with Madame Hugo at the same time that I was enjoying a friendship with her husband. I never thought of my relations with Adèle as anything other than chaste, until one day I came to her house in the afternoon and walked in to find her fixing the combs in her hair. She was standing in front of the big mirror in the drawing room and her back was to me. The combs weren't staying in place. She was impatiently trying to stab her hair into submission when a comb fell out and her black hair cascaded down her back. It was that movement – that soft tumble – softer than water falling from a fountain, that released something in me. I cried out, just a small noise, as a child might make in her sleep. Adèle turned and saw me watching her, and it was as though we had just discovered each other for the first time. I cannot fully explain it. All I know is that I could not roll my feelings back up, twist them into position and secure them into a place of propriety. I was undone. Nothing could be the same.

Later, we sat in the garden, side by side, watching the children play. Adèle was telling me a story about a ring her mother had given her that she always wore on her right hand. I asked to see the ring, thinking that she would allow me to hold her hand while I looked at it, but instead she removed it from her finger and took my hand in her own. She slid the ring onto my finger. It fitted perfectly. We both looked down at it. After a few moments I took the ring off my finger and gave it back to her. She returned it to her own hand. We said not a word.

I lingered as long as I could that day, but I couldn't bear to have Victor return while I was there, and so I left well before supper. Adèle walked me to the door, then to the front gate, then out to the pavement. I turned and waved when I was halfway home and she was still standing there, watching me walk down the street.

The next day I woke relieved that I had not declared myself. I valued my friendship with the Hugos and did not want it disturbed. I would simply live with my new feelings for Adèle. There was no need to tell her about them or acknowledge them in any way. Things would remain as they were.

But I could not concentrate on my work that morning, and the moment I knew that the Hugos would be finishing their noon meal, I was hurrying up their front walk.

I found Adèle alone in the drawing room, sitting with her hands folded on her lap, staring out the window. She leapt up when she saw me. I didn't even have time to announce myself. She was at my side, her hand on my arm.

"The children have gone to the gardens with Victor," she said. "We don't have long." She led me up the stairs and along the hallway towards the bedroom she shared with her youngest daughter, little Adèle.

It felt wrong to lie on the bed where she must have sometimes lingered with Victor, so we lay down on the carpet. The curtains lifted at the window. Adèle put her hands up to my face and traced my forehead, the bones around my eyes, the line from my nose down to my lips. I closed my eyes. I thought that I would die, or that I had already died. I am an ugly man. No one had ever touched me like that.

Adèle rolled on top of me. Her dress rustled like autumn

leaves. I could smell the dust in the carpet.

"My treasure," she said. "My little one. I have been so lonely."
She kissed me. I opened my eyes.

Charles Sainte-Beuve

It is at this point in the story that I should tell you my secret. It
is a secret I have borne all my life with shame, and concealed
from almost everyone. It is at this moment in the story, after all,
that I would be forced to tell Adèle my secret.

But, not yet. Oh, not yet.

~~~~~

Instead, I will tell you something about Victor.

Victor's father was a general in Napoleon's army. His mother, like mine, was the daughter of a sea captain. I thought these were romantic beginnings, but they weren't noble enough for my vainglorious friend. He decided to make his own heraldry, designing a false family crest and having a signet ring made with his invented ancestral motto. *Ego Hugo*. No two words were more perfectly married than those two.

Victor was insatiable in all things, in all ways. And while this worked for him, it was hard on everyone else.

It was proving impossible for Adèle.

So, when I did tell her my secret, that afternoon as we lay together on the floor in the room she shared with her youngest daughter, she was not shocked and surprised, as I thought she'd be.

She welcomed it.

BUT I AM GETTING AHEAD OF MYSELF. I am following not chronology, but passion, rushing off to Adèle whenever I am able, forgetting that there are events in this love story that must be told.

The beginning of it went like this:

In my early days at the *Globe*, when I was only twenty-two, I was given a book of poetry to review, *Odes et ballades* by a Victor Hugo. There was much in it to admire, but also much that irked. The poet was heavy-handed, leaving nothing to subtlety. He revelled in the grotesque and then, strangely enough, put too much emphasis on the trivial. The balance was off. Sometimes he reverted to laziness, using ellipses instead of furthering a thought. But when he freed himself from his own tricks, the poetry soared. I was temperate in my review, but I did use the word "genius". And I meant it.

At this time I was living on the Rive Gauche at number 94 rue de Vaugirard. The day after the review was published, I came home to find a calling card with an invitation from Monsieur Hugo in my letterbox. Coincidentally, Victor Hugo turned out to live just two doors away from me, at 90 rue de Vaugirard.

The next day I called on him in the evening. The Hugos resided in a small second-floor apartment above a joiner's shop. There was the smell of sawdust in the stairwell. Also, the smell of dinner.

"My wife and I are just sitting down," said Victor, when he met me at the door. "Won't you come in and dine with us?"

I had already eaten, had called at the Hugos purposefully late so that I would be certain not to interrupt their meal. But it seemed rude to decline the invitation.

"I'd be delighted," I said, and allowed him to lead me upstairs.

The apartment was crowded but cozy. A fire burned in the grate and there were pleasing paintings and tapestries on the walls. Victor had married his childhood sweetheart and this was their first real home together.

Madame Hugo rose when I entered the apartment. She was dark and tall, almost Spanish looking. I must confess that, apart from bowing to her in greeting, I didn't pay her much attention during the evening. This is partly because she didn't say anything at all during the meal, or afterwards, when the dishes were cleared and the Hugos and I sat by the fire. During dinner her attention seemed entirely taken up with her own thoughts, and after dinner she worked at her sewing, her head bent over her task, ignoring the spirited conversation between her husband and me.

But the larger truth is that it wasn't Adèle's silence that kept me from noticing her that first evening, it was my intoxication with the young poet. He was a few years older than I was but full of vitality and vigour, bounding up the stairs like a mountain goat, as I puffed up after him, my forehead damp with perspiration.

His dedication to poetry was absolute, and his gratitude to me was touching.

"Until your review," he said, "I suffered such doubts."

"But there will always be doubts, will there not?" I do not know of any gifted writer who does not suffer from a constant lack of confidence.

"Yes," said Victor, reaching over and clasping my hand. "But now there will always be your wonderful review to buoy me up when my spirits are low."

Victor Hugo c. 1829

Even though I had eaten two dinners and felt a little queasy by the time I bid farewell to the Hugos just after midnight, I walked the short distance between our two houses in a state of elation. I had a new friend and it seemed a perfect friendship. We were bound by common interests, lived a breath apart, and each could help the other to advance. I would publish reviews of Victor's work, and he could assist me with my own tentative steps towards poetry.

What could be better?

Victor soon introduced me to his circle, a group known as the Cénacle. There were the poets Lamartine and Vigny, the painters Delacroix and Deveria, the young writers, Mérimée, Dumas, and Alfred de Musset. And there was another critic, Gustave Planche. The group used to meet fairly regularly in the library of the Arsenal.

I must confess that I did not talk as much to the painters as to the writers, even in the small group at the Arsenal library. It was not that I was less interested in them. It was as it was when I first went to visit the Hugos at 90 rue de Vaugirard. I was not less interested in Adèle. I was just more interested in Victor.

Of the writers, I remember two in particular.

Alexandre Dumas's father, like Victor's, served in the army under Napoleon. The stories of his father's exploits were the basis for his own popular adventure stories, *The Three Musketeers* and *The Count of Monte Cristo*.

Dumas was fat and loud, alternately breathless and boastful, and frequently chased by creditors. He had a wife and many mistresses, spent money lavishly and foolishly, and made almost as much as he wasted. He was an infrequent participant in the Cénacle, but a chair was always left empty for him as he was apt to rush in midway through one of our evenings, having just dodged a creditor or two on his way over to the library.

You never have to look further than a man's life to understand his work.

Gustave Planche was a literary critic for the *Revue des deux mondes*. Like me, he had been a medical student before entering the world of literature. Later on he would despise Victor's plays as much as I did. We had a great deal in common, and as a result we ignored each other completely. I was secretly afraid that he was a better version of me.

There we were, a small group of talented men, some of us young, and some of us already in our prime. When Victor brought me into the Cénacle he was the least famous among them, apart from the boy, Alfred de Musset. And yet one day he would be the most famous of all.

I shouldn't have to point this out, of course, but seeing how things have gone, I have to. When I first met Victor Hugo, it was I who was the more well known. I was the one who had the reputation.

We were such great friends, Victor and I. When the Hugos moved to nearby Notre-Dame-des-Champs, it seemed natural that I follow them there. You have only to look as far as his family to know with what high esteem I was held by him at the time. His first child, a son, was the embodiment of our friendship and was given the marriage of our two names – Charles Victor.

TO UNDERSTAND MY STORY you must also understand the political turmoil in France at the time. In July of 1830, four years after I met Victor, there was a revolution. It lasted only three days, but it changed the country, and this city.

The infamous 1789 revolution, when we overthrew the monarchy, could still be tasted perhaps, when King Charles X passed two wildly unpopular laws. The first, that a person could be put to death for profaning the Catholic Church. And the second, perhaps more unpopular, that citizens couldn't rightfully inherit property if they, or those they were inheriting from, had been declared "enemies of the revolution". The first revolution.

It is never a good idea to remind people that they have rebelled against a king.

The press was outraged, on behalf of the populace, and many vitriolic articles were published. Charles X then restricted freedom of expression for journalists and newspapers, proclaiming that a newspaper's printing presses could be destroyed if the King decided what it was publishing was treasonous. The *Globe*, of course, was never really at risk of such consequences as we were primarily a literary review. But I helped petition against the censorship. I collected signatures and attended rallies in the public squares.

The King, never a bright sort of man, in my opinion, chose to go boar hunting in the country at the point of greatest unrest in Paris. It was a hot July and the rich were leaving the crowded, unsanitary city if they could.

There was still the taste of insurgence among Parisians. It was no great effort to organize, to fight, to bring down the monarchy in three short days. The shopkeepers closed their doors. The papers printed radical editorials. As their printing presses were being demolished by soldiers, the editors of one newspaper were throwing freshly inked copies from the windows of their offices to the waiting crowd below.

There was the usual violence and destruction of property in the city, but thankfully no works of art were destroyed in the fracas, as had happened in the first revolution. In the end, Charles X abdicated and Louis-Philippe d'Orléans became our king. Restrictions were relaxed. Social reform was in the air. Peace returned.

But let me go back to Victor's terrible play, which opened five months before the revolution. I can still remember every detail of that evening.

Until this year, no drama of romantic sensibility has ever been presented at the Comédie-Française, the Classicists noisily opposing the utterance of lines that deal with the flesh-and-blood nature of passion. Even the actors in Victor's play aren't happy with it. But all the controversy is selling out every house, and making Victor rich. When Adèle and I arrive at the Comédie-Française for the evening performance of *Hernani*, we have to fight our way into the lobby.

Adèle has hooked her arm in mine and I clasp it tightly against me, for fear of losing her to the mob.

"It's like this every night," she says to me, her lips close to my ear. "Victor has never had such publicity."

It is no different in the theatre hall. We have seats in the first balcony. I can look around and easily spot Victor's new bohemian friends, with their long hair and dishevelled clothing. They are in strict contrast to the Classicists, the men, stiff and starched, their top hats in their laps, the women, gowned and bejewelled. There is shouting and hooting. Many of the bohemians are standing in the aisles, trying to intimidate the patrons as they take their seats.

"Why is there a smell of garlic and sausage?" I ask Adèle.

"Some of our supporters have been here since the afternoon," she says, "in order to secure the seats. They've had to bring their supper with them." She shifts closer to me, so that the sides of our bodies are touching. "Charles," she says, "despite the pandemonium, I love how this feels."

I know what she means. I had dressed slowly, dined hastily, come in a carriage to pick up Madame Hugo at her house. We rode to the theatre together, walked through the lobby like man and wife, have taken our seats as though it is the most familiar thing in the world, to be out together of an evening. It is, in fact, the first evening we have done so, and time shakes out its splendid robes before us.

"Thank God for Victor's verbosity," I say. The play is five acts. What with the heckling, we could be here all night.

When the gas lights are dimmed, just before the curtain goes up, Adèle leans over and kisses me on the cheek. Such a simple gesture, and yet the most profound pleasure in the world.

What draws two people together? Is it recognition, shared sympathies? Is it merely an unguarded moment, when they are able to see each other without defences, without reserve? Can one fall into oneself through the attentions of a lover?

Love makes more questions than it answers. But I know this – in those moments with Adèle, I could not imagine feeling more than I did, being other than I was. I could not imagine a world outside our love. What I failed to recognize, perhaps, was that the world we inhabited made no space for us. This night at the theatre, watching Victor's play, would be the only evening we would ever spend entirely together.

~~~~~

I already know, from many conversations with Victor, and from attending an early rehearsal of the play, what *Hernani* is about.

The story takes place in sixteenth-century Spain. It has political overtones, but the drama is essentially a love triangle among the old, senile Don Ruy Gomez, the young nobleman, Hernani, and the woman they both desire, Doña Sol. Gomez is to marry Doña Sol and Hernani is determined to stop the union, even though it has been contractually agreed upon and can't be prevented. This particular cage is rattled constantly throughout the five acts of the play, and it grows tiresome to hear Hernani proclaim his love (yet again) to Doña Sol, and to hear her say (yet again) that she would rather die than marry Don Ruy Gomez. Everything hits the same note, and the melodramatic props – torches, disguises, vaults – don't help matters.

Victor has no subtlety.

But as it turns out, it is a good thing that all the utterances are at such a fevered pitch, otherwise they would be drowned out by the hissing from the Classicists. Practically every speech is interrupted by boos and jeers, and then by the applause and cheering of Victor's bohemian friends. The actors often have to stop, mid-monologue, to let the noise from the audience subside before beginning their lines again.

I try to pay attention to what's happening on the stage. I try to listen to the words, watch the frantic, sometimes farcical actions of the characters. I know that Victor will question me about everything later, and I had better be able to give him some firm opinions. But the truth is that I don't care about the lovers. When Hernani tells Doña Sol (again) of his devotion to her, I want him to shut up. Their relationship is too passive. She is nothing more than a glorified servant, never challenging him, always available to him. She shows much more spirit with Don

Ruy Gomez. I think theirs would be a better marriage.

Maybe because I am in love, other lovers appear fraudulent. Only Adèle and I know the exquisite happiness of true love. Only Adèle and I are fully worthy of its blessing.

That, or Victor can't write a good drama.

"The heckling makes the play seem more interesting than it is," whispers Adèle, in a quiet moment. I squeeze her hand. We are always in such agreement, as though what I am thinking in my head is, in fact, a conversation with her.

At the end of the first act, Hernani declares his desire to kill his rival for the love of Doña Sol.

"My vengeance will guide my dagger to your heart," he says. "Without a sound, it will find its mark."

"Do you think Victor suspects?" I whisper to Adèle.

"Guesses," she says.

"What's the difference?"

"When you suspect, there is evidence. With a guess there is only instinct."

Hernani's speech sends a shiver of apprehension through me nonetheless.

At the intermission we dare not leave our seats in the balcony for fear of having to do battle as we make our way along the aisle. There are people yelling on the stairways and down in the lobby. Their voices lift up to reach us. The circular lobby is its own stage, decorated with pillars, all the stairways leading away from it, like spokes fanning out from the hub of a wheel.

I turn in my seat slightly so that I can look at Adèle. She has turned in her seat to look at me. Sometimes we do this for hours at a time. We cannot seem to get enough of each other. Every little thing is fascinating.

"I love your ears," I say. I can just see the lobes hiding in her hair. They look like pearls.

"I love your eyes," she says.

"I love *your* eyes."

We go on like this, *sotto voce*, until the unruly audience have clambered back into their seats and the lights have mercifully dimmed enough that I can run my hand up the inside of Adèle's thigh, the material of her dress whispering in protest.

She takes my hand, in the dark, and raises it to her mouth, licking each of my fingers slowly and deliberately.

I feel faint, and with my other hand I grip the armrest of my seat to keep from toppling over.

The curtain goes up. The ridiculous action begins again.

The audience appears more spirited after the intermission. I realize they have probably been drinking to fuel their fighting ardour. I suddenly worry about our position near the balcony railing. What if a riot breaks out? We could be thrown over the railing, or trampled to death in our seats. These days, whenever Parisians gather together in a public space, it seems that there is the danger of a riot. I look around nervously.

Hernani gives another tiresome speech about his undying love. A Classicist in the dress circle hurls a cabbage at the stage. Hernani gambols adroitly out of the way. The cabbage lies centre stage and there is a moment when all the actors regard it, as though it possesses miraculous properties, as though it is an oracle they have sudden need to consult.

"Behold the holy cabbage," I say to Adèle, and she giggles.

Hernani continues with his speech, and Doña Sol, with her back to the audience, kicks the cabbage. It rolls slowly, solemnly across the stage and disappears into the wings.

The audience applauds, and even I find myself grinning. Perhaps this is what I will tell Victor, that the actions of the crowd add drama to the play, that the throngs keep the action passionate and spirited. It is not a distraction to have the hecklers, rather it is an enhancement.

Don Ruy Gomez wants to marry Doña Sol to regain his lost youth. He is sympathetic because of this, but towards the end of the play he becomes more and more demonic. It has to be thus, I suppose; he has to be blamed for the fate of the lovers. First, Doña Sol, chained to her destiny as the old man's wife, takes poison, and then Hernani kills himself in response.

"Why doesn't she just run off?" I say, annoyed at Victor's churlishness in killing the lovers. And then something else occurs to me. "Do you think I am meant to be Gomez?"

"If you are anyone, my sweet," Adèle says reassuringly, "you are Doña Sol."

There is a rush on cabs at the front of the theatre after the play, so we decide to walk partway home. I tuck the fact of the lack of cabs away in my mind to be used, if need be, to explain to Victor why we took so long to travel back to Notre-Dame-des-Champs.

Adèle slides her arm through mine. "At last," she says. "We are free of Victor at last."

But we will never be free of Victor, I think. Even this, our wonderful night together, has all been in service to Monsieur Ego Hugo. I will take Adèle home and then spend hours sitting up with Victor analyzing every moment of the evening's performance. I don't know that I can bear this.

"Do you really love me?" I ask, meaning, would you do anything for me, would you leave your family and begin life again with me?

Adèle stops me in the street, takes my face in her hands. "I couldn't love you more," she says. "You set me free. And I especially love you, dear Charles, because you never make undue demands on me."

We walk along the Seine. The river is oily in the moonlight, flexing between its banks like a wild thing. Aside from a few men fishing by lantern, we are the only people walking the cobblestoned streets. It is very dark. I am a little nervous about thieves, and am glad that I am carrying a small mother-of-pearl dagger concealed on my person. Mother, who is more afraid of thieves than I am, insisted upon it.

Adèle pokes me in the ribs. "You're not listening to me," she says.

"Forgive me. I was thinking of how to describe the river." A river I have seen so many times that my familiarity with it seems to lift it beyond description.

"Don't become like Victor," warns Adèle. "He never listens to anything I say either."

I bristle at the comparison. "I am nothing like Victor," I say.

Adèle giggles. "That sounded exactly like Victor," she says.

I am in a bad humour by the time we get into a cab at the Pont Neuf.

But Adèle reaches across me, pulls down the window blinds so that we're hidden from the driver and the people on the streets. She squeezes my knee. I grab for her breasts. We fall clumsily into each other, our first kiss missing completely.

My churlishness vanishes. The rock of the cab is the sway of our bodies is the rhythm of my heart rocking in its carriage of bone. The invisible streets pass by. Adèle is undoing the buttons on my trousers. I have forgotten my words for the river. I am only here. And love opens me.

THERE IS AN ORCHARD in the Jardin du Luxembourg where we like to walk. Sometimes we have the children with us, but I prefer it when we are alone, when we are not worried about whether an errant touch or a stolen kiss will be reported, innocently enough, to Victor.

There are hundreds of apple trees in the orchard, and we like to play a game with the names of the different varieties, grouping them into categories. Often we choose a category before we get to the orchard.

"Animals," says Adèle today.

It is a beautiful late spring afternoon. We are blessedly without the children today. We walk between the trees languidly, our hands brushing against each other, the heat from our two bodies the same temperature as the air that surrounds us. Adèle looks to the left, and I look to the right, reading the names written on the tags at the base of the trees.

"Dog's Snout," I say, triumphantly.

"Sheep's Head," she says.

It takes a while to find another animal name. I pull her off the path, kiss her deeply. She runs her hands down my back. Someone wanders past and we break apart.

"Mouse," she says. "Catshead."

"Mermaid," I say.

"A mermaid isn't an animal."

"It's half animal."

"Half fictional animal."

"Miller's Thumb," I say.

"That's a man."

"Man is an animal."

Adèle strokes my arm. "You are hopeless," she says.

We walk through the orchard. We move through other subjects.

"Love," says Adèle.

This time I'm the one who wins.

"Perpetuelle," I say. "Fail Me Never. Open Heart. Everlasting."

She is left with First and Last, and the rather dubious Neversink.

"Never sink," she says, dramatically clasping me around the waist. "Float, my sweet darling. Float! Float!"

We pause before the label on a slender tree.

"Why would you want to eat an apple with that name?" I ask.

The tree bears the tag Great Unknown.

"Maybe it's a description of the taste," says Adèle.

"Surely they could be more specific than that." I imagine this apple-namer as a man of melancholy nature, someone who has lost faith in words and yet is still expected to attach them to meaning. But who would propose a name like this? Wouldn't they just ask someone else to name the apple more appropriately?

"I wish we could eat one," says Adèle. But the blossom has just faded, and the apples aren't yet growing on the tree. We won't be able to taste the Great Unknown until the autumn.

We walk in silence for a while, although I keep looking at the names on the trees. We have just over an hour before Adèle has to return home. This is not long enough to go to the small hotel where we sometimes manage an entire exquisite afternoon – if we are lucky. Our life together is broken into different locales, depending on how much time we have to spend. The geography of our love corresponds absolutely to the clock.

Increasingly, I feel despair when I think of our future. I

don't know how we are to resolve this problem of not having enough time together. Some days I entertain the idea of telling Victor. Would friendship be able to triumph over adultery? On the days when I am feeling happy and optimistic, this seems entirely possible. On the days when I despair, like today, I fear Victor would kill me if he knew of his wife's affair with me. Certainly he would challenge me to a duel and, since he is more robust, a better sportsman, and likely to be filled with moral outrage and vitriol – he would probably kill me with his first shot.

"I wish that we had time to go to our hotel," says Adèle. "Or that we could be naked here, under the trees." She squeezes my hand, and I manage a smile. Each time I drift away from her, she manages to snag me back, and I am so grateful for that, so grateful for her. I mustn't poison what we have by thinking of the future. I close my eyes briefly. I can smell the last of the blossom, a perfume so clean and sweet that it is hard to imagine anything more perfect.

The names of the apples that I like best are the simple names. I find them more profound than the poetic ones, because I imagine the simple titles bear witness to the places or the circumstances where the apples were first found.

River. Sunrise. Field. Day. Sunset. Star. Hunger.

"If you could name an apple," I ask Adèle, "what would you call it?"

I think she will pick a flowery name, something poetic that makes a tangle in the mouth. But she answers swiftly, as though she was thinking of the question long before I asked it.

"I would call it after you," she says.

"Charles?"

"No, not Charles," she says. "Your other name. Charlotte."

I ARRIVE FIRST AND TAKE A SEAT near the back of the church. It is afternoon. The building is empty except for me, and my slightest movement echoes loudly in the cavernous chamber. The pew is uncomfortable and when I shift on the hard wooden bench the rustle of my skirts can be heard throughout the vaulted room.

When our time is short and the day is a good one, Adèle and I meet in the orchard. When our time is short, and the weather is inclement, we meet in the church. Today it is rainy and cool outside, and the unheated church feels damp. So much easier to believe in God when the sun is shining and the stained glass window shuffles its colours over the grey stone and dark wood interior.

I like arriving first. I like the anticipation of waiting for Adèle, the sound of the heavy doors creaking open, her quick footsteps on the stone floor. I like watching her walk down the aisle towards me, her face flushed from hurrying. That first moment, when she looks for me and finds me is a moment I never tire of witnessing. That moment of recognition is one of the most satisfying in life. The instant that a lover seeks you out. The instant of understanding something, of working out the answer to a problem that has been puzzling you for some time. The moment when something suddenly becomes clear.

This church is not the closest one to Notre-Dame-des-Champs where Adèle and I live. We cannot risk going to the church in our own neighbourhood. It is not that we fear meeting Victor, as he is rarely inside a church, but more that we fear meeting someone who knows Victor and Adèle. And that church is the one in which Victor and Adèle were married. So we frequent this modest church, many streets away, where we are fairly certain we will not be discovered. But even then, we take precautions. We come in the middle of the afternoon when the church will be empty. And I come dressed as a woman.

You might think this is the secret I was referring to earlier, but this is not it. Dressing as a woman to rendezvous with Adèle is simply strategy. Two women in a church are not given a second thought, a second glance. Two women can sit close together on the same pew, can walk down the street with their arms linked, and arouse no suspicion. They will not be thought of as lovers. They will merely be two friends who are out enjoying the city together.

I borrow my mother's clothes. As she lives temporarily with me, it is not difficult for me to take a dress or two from her wardrobe and return them before she has noticed their absence. I look remarkably like my mother, with my high forehead and my delicate features, and I make a convincing woman. Sometimes I wonder if Victor did see us together, whether he would be able to tell that his wife's new friend was, in fact, his old friend. It is tempting to put this to the test, but part of my being a convincing woman is that I act the role with confidence and I fear that I would lose my nerve in the presence of Victor, that I would falter, and that he would discover my true identity.

I like being a woman. There is a freedom in it that I find a relief. No one is going to challenge me to a duel. If I say something out of turn I will be ignored or forgiven for my outburst, not expected to pace twenty steps into the under-growth with a loaded pistol. I like walking on the inside of the street, not out by the gutter which runs with sewage. I like being helped up into a cab, having doors held open for me, having men doff their hats to me in the avenue. I like the whisper of my skirts, the feel of them in my hands when I gather them up in a knot to step over a muddy patch of ground. I look much better in a woman's hat than I do in a man's. My small hands were made for soft leather gloves that button up the forearm with tiny pearl buttons.

Often I prefer being Charlotte to Charles, and the surprising thing is that I think Adèle prefers this too. With Charles she has to feel the guilt of adultery, the shame that she is cuckolding her husband, breaching her marriage vows. With Charlotte she can pretend that theirs is simply an innocent friendship. She is sometimes much more light-hearted with Charlotte.

There is the heavy toll of the church door swinging shut. I turn in my seat and see Adèle. She stands there for a moment, at the back of the church, with the last bit of light from the day outside fleeing behind her. She is dressed in dark colours, as she frequently is when she meets me here, as though simply to enter the church is an act of mourning.

It does not take her long to find me in the dim interior. She hurries up the aisle and slides into the pew where I am sitting, hurling herself towards me with a recklessness that I find so touching. All my words dissolve to feeling and it takes ages for them to struggle back into shape.

"Charlotte," she says, "you look so lovely. I have missed you so much."

We haven't seen each other for five full days. The separation has seemed eternal.

"Charlotte," she says. "I want you so badly. I could take you right here, right now." She runs a hand across the front of my dress and a small moan escapes my lips.

At first when we met in the church we spent some of the time in prayer. Adèle is more religious than I am and she believed that by increasing her devoutness she would alleviate some of the guilt she felt at having an affair. By praying more,

by praying harder, by having prayer be a large part of our relationship, she would be forgiven the sin of adultery. We would
kneel together in the pew, heads bowed and hands clasped in
front of us. I don't know what silent words she offered up to
God, but I know I prayed, with all my strength, that she would
leave Victor and come away with me. I feared that our prayers
were cancelling each other out. She was probably asking to
fight temptation. I was begging to have her yield to it.

Now I lean my head on her shoulder. She still smells of the
outdoors, hasn't taken on the musty perfume of the church. I
feel weak with longing.

In the orchard, if we are lucky, we are able to hold hands,
to manage several kisses while walking through the groves of
trees. In the hotel, we can be entirely ourselves, without clothes
or pretence or observers. The church has more privacy than
the orchard, but it is the house of the Lord and comes with
his attendant laws. In the orchard we can pretend that we are
courting. In the hotel we can pretend that we are married. In
the church we know that we are sinners.

That knowledge does not entirely encourage romance.

Do lovers always suffer an impediment to their love? Is
that what keeps love sweet and strong – the circumstances that
would force the lovers apart make them cleave together more
keenly? Will we end up poisoning ourselves, like the lovers in
Victor's wretched play? What other choice will there be? We
cannot be together, and yet we cannot be apart.

"We should pray," Adèle says, without conviction.

But we don't pray. I lift my head from her shoulder and
take her face in my hands, kiss her deeply and passionately. The
church recedes, disappears. There is only the mix of our breath,
the feel of Adèle's skin, our kiss. Love is a kind of attentiveness,
I think. And yet, love also renders the world outside the lovers
invisible, without consequence.

Adèle breaks away first. "I want you so badly," she says. "I'm not to be trusted." She entwines her fingers in mine. "I will think up a lie for tomorrow. We must go to the hotel for the afternoon. Can you get away?"

I am meant to be at the newspaper tomorrow, but I will work up an excuse not to go. Perhaps I will be ill. I do feel ill.

"Yes," I say. "Can you manage to escape for a whole afternoon?"

"I must."

The thought of the pleasures of the hotel room makes me squirm on the hard wooden bench. Adèle tightens her grip on my hand.

"I'm sorry," she says.

"For what?"

"For causing you pain. For not marrying you instead of Victor."

"But you didn't know me when you married Victor."

"I'm sorry anyway."

This is what happens in the church. Prayer and wish are entwined, and it becomes impossible to prise them apart. There is a strong need to confess.

"You wouldn't have had your children," I say, "if you had married me."

"I love you more than my children," says Adèle. Her words resound through the empty church, and we are both shocked into silence by what she has just said.

It strikes me that Adèle has more courage than I do. I have been looking at our future through the filter of my character. I would do better to regard it through the filter of hers. If she can say a thing like that, then she is capable of more than I supposed. She is capable of more than I am. She will have the strength to find a way for us to go forward.

IT HAS BECOME IMPOSSIBLE to meet with Adèle. There has been an outbreak of cholera in the city and it is unwise to leave one's house as the streets are full of infection – these same streets whose raw sewage caused the outbreak. It is said that two thousand people died on one day alone last week. Hearses prowl the avenues, more numerous than horse and cab. All manner of wagons and carts have been pressed into service to carry the hapless dead to the overcrowded cemeteries. Grave-diggers are reportedly jumping on the corpses to squash them down and make room for the freshly dead. I wouldn't be surprised to learn that, in the haste to halt the spread of the disease, people are being buried alive.

The pianist Liszt is apparently playing Beethoven's funeral march in the salons of Paris. There are funeral processions day and night. I lie in bed and listen to the horses' hoofs on the cobblestones, the creak of wagons loaded with bodies rolling past my windows.

It is too dangerous to go out. The Cénacle has suspended its meetings.

I would risk my life to walk the small distance between my house and the Hugos', but I cannot risk Adèle's life. So I wait – two weeks, three – each day a torment, each night an unspeakable agony. I wait, for the epidemic to rise and crest, burst its banks and, finally, subside.

~~~~~

We use an inexpensive, rather sordid hotel, to avoid the moral judgement of the proprietor, but I fear we suffer it anyway. It has been my observation that people like to feel superior, that it is a natural inclination to want to feel you are better than someone else. So, when we sign the hotel register as man and wife there is invariably a raised eyebrow, or a moment's hesitation before we are handed the brass fob with the key on it. Our time of assignation doesn't help. We always come to the hotel in the afternoon and leave in the early evening. Lovers are betrayed by the hours they must keep.

I ask for a room on a high floor at the back, as far away from the street as possible, because it is quieter and more private. Also, the higher floors are less popular because of the climb up the stairs, so it is unlikely that we will have neighbours.

The wooden stairs have shallow dents in them from years of footsteps shuffling up and down. Some days I find this a comfort, that some of those feet will have belonged to other lovers, that Adèle and I are not the only ones who have used this hotel to rendezvous. But other days I find this depressing. All those years. All those people moving up and down the staircase, moving through the rooms of this hotel. Their love unremembered.

Sometimes, when we are lying naked in the bed of our rented room, I think of all the other couples who have been in the room for the same purpose. What happened to them? What happened to their love? I wish there were a private registry of the lovers who frequented each room; a listing of two names – names that were not permitted to be joined together in any other circumstance. At least something would then remain to remind us of the lovers, to remind us that they loved.

Adèle and I contribute to this private registry by signing our names in each of the rooms we stay in. Our joined signatures, small and discreet, behind a picture, or under the washstand. Charles and Adèle. Invisible, but there nonetheless, if you choose to look.

Today we have been given a room on the fourth floor. The narrow stairs curl up and up. We have to walk in single file. We struggle up, pausing for breath at each landing. By the time we reach the room we are hot and irritable. I fling the door open. Adèle stumbles across the threshold.

In the Hôtel Saint-Paul, the rooms on the higher floors have lower ceilings than the rooms on the first and second floor. But the ceilings are timbered, and this makes up for their lack of height. This room, like all the others we have stayed in, has a bed against one wall, a washstand against another, a small desk, and a window that looks down over the roof and courtyard of the Collège Royal Saint-Louis.

Adèle collapses on the bed, still struggling for breath. It occurs to me, rather meanly, that she's grown stouter of late. I stare moodily out the window, not feeling very loving. And yet I have waited an entire month for this afternoon in the hotel.

"Well?" says Adèle. She has propped herself up on her elbows, stares across the room at me. "Are you going to stand there all day?"

Perhaps I love Adèle better in absentia? There is nothing finer than imagining our time together in this hotel room, but now that we're actually here I feel paralyzed by my expectations. Why is love so difficult, so changeable? Why am I caught so easily in its tides and currents? Why can't I steer the craft of my own desire?

"I am a boat," I say to Adèle.

"What?"

"I am a dark boat cast down the dark length of the river."

She giggles. "You are an idiot," she says. "Do I have to come over there to make you love me?"

Adèle's body and my body are similarly plump. We are just over thirty, but our figures are decidedly middle-aged. Adèle's figure has not been helped by giving birth to five children. (Of these, four are living, one having died shortly after he was born.) My figure is not helped by my predilection for sweets and my aversion to exercise. Adèle said once that we look better clothed, and I would have to agree with her. But, that said, there is something wonderfully liberating about removing my clothes in the middle of the afternoon to lie naked with my lover in a rented hotel room.

It puts me in a better humour, for one thing.

We lie on our backs, naked, holding hands tightly, as though we are survivors from a shipwreck, floating on a makeshift raft over the stormy seas while waiting to be rescued. We are too shy to look at each other, too shy to give full expression to our desire. We have waited so long to be together like this that the fact we are actually here takes some getting used to.

"If you could change one thing in this room," says Adèle, "what would it be?"

"The room itself," I say. "I would have it be our room in our house, not a room in a hotel."

"How would you decorate it?"

"New wallpaper." The flowered wallpaper in this room is so old that it is flayed into strips in places. "Better furniture. A four-poster bed with a curtain around it so we could block out the world."

"But if it was our room, we would have no need to block out the world."

This seems so impossible to me that I cannot properly imagine it.

"Flowers," I say, continuing with our game. "I would fill it with bouquets of fresh flowers."

"I would make it much larger," says Adèle. And then, remembering the climb up the staircase, she adds, "And I would move it down a floor or two."

The streaky light from the window catches the dust drifting through the air. The bed linen feels scratchy from over-zealous washing. I roll over on my side and Adèle rolls over as well, so that we are facing each other.

"I am writing some poems about us," I say. "About our love. About you." I say this tentatively because I know that she has often been the subject of Victor's love poetry and that she tires of being his inspirational material. "Do you mind?"

Adèle strokes my cheek. "No," she says. "Make use of me, sweet Charles. Make use of me." She slides her hand down to my chest, down my stomach, down through the patch of hair surrounding my sex.

And here, right here, I must stop the story for a moment.

It is now that I must tell you my secret.

I WAS NOT ALWAYS A WRITER, as I said. When I was a young man I trained as a doctor, went for four long years to medical school, studied anatomy and dissection with the same avid attention I now turn to reading and writing.

I think I first became interested in medicine because I wanted an explanation for my body. I wanted to unlock the mystery of myself. My mother, when I was young and she was bathing me, had simply said that all men were *different* in that area. When I found the answer, in the medical library, in the study of a corpse who had the same condition as myself, I lost some of my interest in becoming a doctor and left the academy before I was fully qualified.

I believe that every man and every woman has a secret, and life is first about naming that secret, and then about making peace with it. Adèle's secret is me – or rather it is the fact that she is unhappy in her marriage to Victor. Victor's secret is his desire for a noble birth, which is at odds with his other desire, to express the sentiments of the lowest common man through his writings.

My secret is more visible than both of these – more visible, and more complicated.

I have the sex organ of a man, although it is very small and incapable of becoming erect. I have the sex organ of a man, but on the underside I have what resembles the sex organ of a woman. The medical texts refer to the condition as hypospadias, an affliction that is linked to hermaphrodism.

Mine is a more extreme case than some, and there is no cure for it. I was born with this condition and I will die with it, and in between I must find a way to make peace with it.

I cannot impregnate a woman. I cannot have what the doctors would call "normal" relations with a woman. But I have finally found a woman who does not want this *normality* anyway. Adèle is sick of being impregnated by Victor. She wants love without complications and, strangely enough, the complication of my body is the simplest of joys for her. She wants both Charles and Charlotte. More important, she desires both Charles and Charlotte.

My sex is no bigger than a working man's thumb. Adèle can completely cover it with her hand. It lolls against her palm, and she strokes it gently, as though it is her strange, small pet.

The dust swirling about the room seems to be broken bits of light. Adèle runs her tongue over my nipples. I arch my back. One of my hands is in her hair, and the other reaches back to touch the tattered wallpaper behind the headboard. If I keep my hand on the wall it seems possible that I will keep myself from floating up off the bed, that I will keep myself attached to earth.

Adèle lowers her mouth to my sex. It fits so comfortably. I try to stop from crying out, and then I don't and my wails fill the small room and overflow into the hallway, out through the window and into the blue bank of the sky.

What breaks from me in love is sorrow. Waves of it roil over me, and when I lie beached on the bed afterwards, I feel that I have been made new again, that I have been washed clean.

Adèle lies back on the sheets. Her hands grip the top of the headboard. I have a hand on her breast, for balance really, although I am pretending otherwise, tweak her nipple absentmindedly whenever I remember. My other hand is inside her. She has her eyes closed. Her breath is ragged. The bed knocks rhythmically against the wall as I fuck her.

What is a man? What is a woman? Is it the sex, the clothes, the customs? I am never more of a man than I am in this moment, and yet there are many who wouldn't call me a man at all.

You just have to be committed to a position and maintain it throughout. That's the other secret I know. Commitment begs surrender.

"I won't let Victor have me," says Adèle. We are wrapped around each other. I have one of her legs between my own. Her hands are on my back.

"He can't be happy about that."

"I couldn't bear it. I tell him that it's because I can't get pregnant again, that I don't want to have any more children."

The sun at the window has changed. There's a smoky quality to the light. It must be late afternoon. We will have to leave this room soon, make our separate journeys back to Notre-Dame-des-Champs.

"That can't last," I say, meaning, this can't last, that these moments we have are not enough to weigh against Adèle's life with Victor. We will disappear like all the other lovers who have used this small room. Our love will not be remembered.

But I couldn't be more wrong.

I TRY TO LUNCH WITH MOTHER every day. This isn't always possible. Sometimes I must attend meetings at the newspaper, but most days I manage to leave the *Globe* offices at noon and return by two o'clock.

Luncheon with Mother is both reassuring and infuriating because it is always the same. Not the food, but the routine.

I have a key to Mother's new house on rue du Montparnasse and I let myself in rather than waiting for the housekeeper to open the door for me. The housekeeper is old, older than Mother. I have pointed out, repeatedly, that perhaps this is not such a good idea, but Mother will have none of it. She is fond of her elderly housekeeper. Her elderly and mostly deaf housekeeper. This is another reason why I don't ring the bell to Mother's house, but let myself in with my own key.

I shake out my umbrella, if it is raining, and put it in the umbrella stand in the hall. I remove my coat and hat and hang them on one of the wooden pegs above the red embroidered bench. I go upstairs. Mother likes to sit in the sunny room at the front of the house on the second floor, and I know that I will find her there. Invariably I meet the housekeeper, either in the foyer, or on the staircase, or sometimes in the upstairs hallway. Because she is mostly deaf, she doesn't hear me and I often startle her. Then she shrieks. Sometimes she drops whatever she is carrying. The housekeeper's shriek announces my arrival, and Mother shuffles out of her sitting room to reprimand me.

"Must you," she says, as though I am four years old and have been pulling the tail of the house cat.

My upsetting the housekeeper upsets Mother, and my being scolded by her upsets me, so we always sit down to lunch in a foul temper. The first course is eaten in silence. But eating improves both of our moods, as does a glass of wine, and by the second course, lamb chops, we are ready to converse. I always think I have given up trying to impress Mother, but it never appears to be so.

"My reviews are becoming even more popular," I say. "I get so many letters about them that it's hard to respond to all my admirers."

Mother's eyes glaze over with boredom.

I try shorthand.

"I'm very popular," I say. "More than ever."

"Did you notice whether the baker on the corner has that nice bread I like in the window?" asks Mother. "He doesn't make it every day, and I'm never sure which day he does make it."

I spend a moment separating the meat from the bone on the chop.

"Tuesday?" says Mother. "Or is it Wednesday? What day is it today, Sainte-Beuve?"

"Thursday."

"Oh, perhaps it's Thursday then."

"It is Thursday."

"The bread, the bread. Perhaps he makes it only on Thursdays."

It is a great shame that my father is dead, that he died before I knew him. I have to believe that he was possessed of a brain, and that my intellect comes from him. There is nothing remotely intellectual about Mother. Nobody was ever so obsessed with the trivial and the meaningless as Mother. And yet she is all I have. I stab at my potatoes. There seem to be bits of dirt on my lunch, as though the food was dropped and then hastily shoved back onto the plate. Perhaps the housekeeper is losing her eyesight as well as her hearing.

I look over at Mother. She's finished her food already and is picking at something on the tablecloth. She is a much better eater than I am, altogether more robust. I suddenly feel like weeping and have to dab at my eyes with my napkin.

Luckily, the housekeeper usually comes in to clear when I am having my emotional moment, and I am distracted from my feelings by her rough handling of the crockery and silver.

After the meal is over, I sit with Mother in the sunny front room on the second floor and we have coffee. If Mother can be stopped from commenting on what objects the sun is shining on, or how sore her feet get in winter, or whether Madame Lamarche will recover from her illness, she will sometimes ask after my health, or express concern that I am not dressing warmly enough for the weather, or tell me that someone has told her that it seems I am clever. In these moments everything is forgiven and redeemed, and there is suddenly the desire to do this whole performance over again the very next day.

Sometimes, when I am shrugging on my coat in the foyer and I look back up the stairs, I see Mother standing on the landing, watching me go. She doesn't wave or call out, and I don't either. I simply put on my coat and hat, collect my gloves and umbrella, and step out into the Paris afternoon. But it is in these moments that I feel we are most aligned, that Father's early death shipwrecked us both and we cling to this little raft of habit to stay afloat. It is not the vessel either of us hoped or expected to make our voyage on, and yet here we are and there is the desire, in both of us, to make the best of it.

ADÈLE AND I WALK THROUGH the Montparnasse cemetery. This is not one of our regular haunts, but today there is not enough time to journey to the church, or the hotel, and Victor has taken the children to the Jardin du Luxembourg, so we cannot risk a visit to the orchard.

The cemetery is close to our houses on Notre-Dame-des-Champs. It is where I myself will be buried. Mother has already reserved our spaces. Adèle and I walk along the paths between the rows of raised stone tombs, and the thought of my dead self makes me greedy for life.

I grab my beloved, but she twists away.

"Someone might see," she says. There are indeed other people in the cemetery, and because the graves block their presence they are apt to pop up suddenly in front of us on the path.

"Passion must have no regrets," I say.

"Passion is nothing *but* regrets," says Adèle.

In the beginning I had fantasized about seducing Adèle. I had thought that, with my clever words and my sensitive nature, I would slowly persuade her to yield to me. My attentions would ripen her like a fruit and she would drop easily into my hands. But really, from the beginning, Adèle has controlled the tempo of our love. She is not a ripe fruit. She is not easily swayed by my words. If she does not want my touch while we walk through the cemetery, then she will not have it.

But I am a better man only in my mind. My body simply longs for her, and it is the stronger force.

"We will be dead soon," I say. "Encased in stone, like all these good people." I wave my hand over the graves. "I'm sure they all thought they had longer to love."

Adèle links her arm in mine. "You, dear Charles," she says, "will have more than just a simple grave. You will have a grand statue."

"It won't be as big as Victor's," I say.

Adèle laughs at me. "Well," she says, "perhaps it will be a good deal prettier."

We walk on in silence.

"Boulanger wants to paint me," she says after a while.

Louis Boulanger is a friend of Victor Hugo's. He has already done a portrait of the great poet.

"What did you say?"

"I refused."

"Why? Boulanger is a good painter. The portrait would be pleasing."

Adèle stops me on the path. "I want no other portrait," she says, "than the one engraved on my lover's heart."

I always think that *I* am the poet, that it is the power of *my* words that moves our love forwards. But really, sometimes I must be honest. Adèle is often a much better wordsmith than I am.

I have not seen the man before. He storms into my office at the *Globe*, practically frothing at the mouth.

"Sainte-Beuve, I challenge you to a duel," he shouts. Not another duel!

"What for?"

"You have rejected my poems."

He is a very young man, the first flush of youth lighting his face. He stands across from me. We are separated only by my oak desk. I don't remember his poems.

"Come now," I say. "If you submitted them for publication, surely you entertained the idea that they might be rejected."

"I did not."

"Well, I must have said something encouraging." I am in the habit of mixing the good with the bad, of turning someone down, but letting him know what it is he got right.

"You called them *trifling*. You said they were *weak*." Just the memory of my cruel note causes the young man to mop the sweat from his brow.

Well then, they must have been truly terrible, I think.

There was recently a much publicized duel involving a poet. Perhaps this young man has been inspired to take action because of that. The bullet that killed that poet passed through his manuscript, which he had tucked inside his waistcoat. His poems were published posthumously, with a blank space left on each page, in the middle of the words, to show where the bullet had sliced through the manuscript en route to the poet's heart. Perhaps posthumous publication is what this poet hopes for.

"This is ridiculous," I say. "I don't want to fight you. I was entirely within my rights to reject your poems."

"You have disgraced me," says the young man. "They were poems to my beloved. They were my most secret thoughts, and you scorned them. Choose your weapon." He shouts this last part, and I can see, through the open door behind him, the heads of my colleagues turning towards us with interest.

And then I do remember his poems. He compared his love to a fleet of ships setting sail for the New World. He compared his love to a budding tree. In one terrible poem he compared his love to a wingless dove. I remember that the manuscript itself had bits of food stuck to one of the pages, and that on another page there was a boot print. The grammar was appalling. The word use was juvenile. The whole thing was such an amateur effort that a child of six could have done a better job.

How dare this idiot march into my office in the middle of

the day, demanding revenge for my honest criticism!

"If you can't take rejection, you are no poet," I say.

"Choose your weapon."

"All right." I lean across my desk, looking him in the eye, staring him down. "I choose spelling. You're dead."

When I get home that evening there is a note from Victor, summoning me to the house. I am in a panic about what it might mean. I have been avoiding Victor and he must have noticed. He must have found out about Adèle and me, and he is calling me over to hand me a loaded pistol. We will stomp out to his back garden and he will shoot me through the heart by the pond.

By the time I get to their house I am sweating profusely. My hair sticks to my forehead, which sticks to my hat. There are big wet patches under the arms of my waistcoat.

I don't feel that I can just walk into the Hugo household any more. My intimacy with Adèle has meant that I compensate for the guilt by becoming more formal with Victor. So, I stand on the front step and knock loudly. It takes a while before someone comes, and it is not the maid who answers the door, but one of the children.

Victor is in the parlour. Adèle, thank God, is nowhere to be seen. The room is a mess, packing crates sit in the centre of the rug and pictures are off the walls.

"What's happening?" I ask.

"We're being evicted." Victor motions me into the room. "We have to move."

"But why?"

"It seems that our landlord is conservative and was very offended by *Hernani*."

"But he didn't have to go to the play."

Victor waves his hand over an open packing crate, as though

he's about to conjure a rabbit from it. "The talk, Charles," he says. "The talk of what happens each night at the play is all over town. One doesn't need to actually go to the play to know what is going on."

I suppose this is true. I have been so concerned with my own life lately that I have forgotten all about Victor's play and the controversy surrounding it.

I collapse into a chair. "Where will you go?"

"We've taken an apartment on rue Jean-Goujon."

"But that's on the other side of the river." Rue Jean-Goujon is a small street near the Champs-Elysées, but it may as well be the other side of the world.

"I need to be close to the theatre." Victor looks at me shrewdly. "And, Charles," he says, "I have not seen much of you lately. I thought, in fact, you might be avoiding me."

"Why would I do that?"

"Yes, why *would* you do that?"

"You were writing your novel," I say weakly.

Adèle has told me that Victor has become obsessed with Notre-Dame Cathedral, and that he is writing a story set there. He lives in his room and only comes out at night, when he walks to the church. She has told me that he requests his meals be delivered to his room, that he writes standing up at a tall desk, wrapped dramatically in a cloak.

Victor kneels in front of me, takes both of my hands in his, as though he is about to propose marriage. "Charles," he says. "What is wrong? We have been such good friends and now I feel that I hardly know you."

It is the touch that does it. If he had not knelt before me and taken my hands I might have been able to withstand the shock of the Hugos' move across the river. But the touch undoes me. I feel compelled to confess. I suddenly remember our friendship and I want to tell Victor everything.

"I'm in love with Adèle," I say. "She is in love with me. We have been seeing one another for about a year."

Victor drops my hands, leaps to his feet. "What do you mean?"

I think of the hotel room where Adèle and I so recently were, how I have not bathed since that afternoon because I do not want to wash her touch from my body.

"I mean," I say, "that I have been having physical relations with your wife."

Victor looks shocked, and I realize that he has not suspected us at all. I shouldn't have confessed.

"You?" he says. "You and Adèle?"

Oh, it is too late to take any of it back. I said it without regret. I said it a little boastfully, and now I can see that it was a mistake to admit it. Adèle and I could have continued for years without Victor finding out. Why did I grace him with more interest in his wife than I know he has? Victor is happy sequestered in his room, writing his book about the cathedral. That is his world. Adèle and I, and his children, we exist at the outer edge of that. There was no need to tell Victor. He would never have discovered us. We could have gone on for years, quite happily.

Adèle will be furious with me. Victor will make her life impossible. Why did I think only of myself and not consider her?

"I'm lying," I say, desperate to turn this around. "It's a joke. Ha ha." I laugh weakly. It comes out sounding like a dog barking. A very small dog.

"No. You're not lying." Victor is frowning, probably remembering all the times I have been alone with his wife. He slaps his forehead with his great paw. "I encouraged you," he shouts. "I believed we were all friends." A shadow passes over his face as he realizes perhaps the greatest indignity of all. "I sent you to see my play together!"

~~~~~

Victor and I drink a bottle of wine in the parlour, using one of the packing cases as a table for our glasses.

"I have never had a mistress," says Victor. "I have only ever loved my wife."

This surprises me. I know that the great Victor Hugo has many female admirers. I would have thought he'd take full advantage of that adulation.

"I'm sorry," I say, although I am mostly sorry that I have told him.

Victor swirls the wine around the inside of his glass. "Do you know the story of my wedding?" he asks.

"No," I lie. Adèle has told me of the whole miserable day, has said that she should have taken it as an omen of what was to come and run screaming from the church.

"Adèle and I had played together as children. We had known each other all of our lives. It was natural that I would marry her. I loved her, and I know she loved me. But at our wedding, as we were saying our vows to each other, my brother Eugene jumped up and proclaimed *his* love for Adèle." Victor pours himself another drink. He is drinking at twice the rate I am. "Naturally, I was shocked. I hadn't known of his feelings, and I can't think why he chose that moment to disclose them. It was terrible. He had to be dragged from the church and immediately imprisoned in the asylum."

"Terrible," I say, nodding sympathetically.

Victor slaps his glass down on top of the packing case, making me jump in my chair.

"Why does this happen to me again?" he cries.

"I'm not insane," I point out, but he isn't listening to me. He starts to pace up and down the room.

"Why am I being tested in this way?" he says. "What is the point of this torment?"

I don't think that torment often has much of a point, but I keep my mouth shut.

Victor is over by the window now. He is shaking the drapes. Great clouds of dust rise from them.

"I must not be destroyed by this tragedy," he shouts. "I must find a way to do battle with my enemy."

Here it comes, I think. Here comes the challenge to a duel. Here comes my final hour. But Victor, having finished wrestling with the drapes, strides back over to the packing case, drinks the rest of his wine, and sits down in the chair opposite mine.

"How could you?"

I don't say anything.

Victor buries his head in his hands and mumbles something I can't hear.

"What?"

"She was my wife, Charles. My wife." He raises his head and looks straight at me, his eyes bright with feeling.

I decide not to comment on the fact that he has used the past tense in speaking about Adèle. What can it mean? Is he done with her? Will she be free to live with me now? I am exhilarated by the results of my confession. It was the right thing to do after all!

Victor leans across and alarmingly takes one of my hands in both of his.

"I will conquer this, Charles," he says.

"You will?"

"Friendship can transcend adultery."

"It can?"

"We will not let this affect us. We will go on as before." He slaps me on the shoulder and I spill some of my wine. "We will speak no more of this. Your affair with my wife will end. You and I will be better friends than ever. I will have words with Adèle."

~ ~ ~ ~ ~

59

Portrait of Madame Victor Hugo by Louis Boulanger

The next morning a package arrives at my house. It is from Adèle. I recognize her handwriting. I slip the string from the parcel, rip open the paper. There is no letter inside, just a folded piece of white lace. For a moment I don't know what it is, but when I unfold it I can see that it is a veil. Adèle has sent me her wedding veil.

ADELE

HE COMES TO THE HOUSE. We go to the gardens. We meet in the church. We meet at the hotel. I am always running, always late, skirts in hand and breathless.

I lie to Victor. I lie to the children. I lie to myself. He's just a friend. It is just a friendship that has blossomed out of season. Unexpected, but a gift, and something to treasure, not cut down.

The lies only go so far. Victor is easy to deceive because he does not believe me capable of adultery. I tell my sister my secret, and I use her as my excuse. Victor does not question my new and fervent interest in spending time with Julie, although he does get annoyed if I leave the children too long in his care.

The children accept whatever I tell them. They do not doubt me. They have no cause. I adore them and they know it, and they have little interest in anything beyond this.

No, it is the lies I tell myself that are the trouble. Because, of course, I know that they are lies.

Once, when I was young, I ran after my sister through the woods. The branches snagged my clothing and caught my hair. The hem of my skirts dragged in the mud. I felt both that I was moving as fast as a bird in the sky, and that I was trapped in the forest cage. When I burst out into a clearing, my sister still ahead of me, I threw myself onto the grass with such relief at being both stopped and free, and just lay there, face down, until Julie turned back to look for me.

This is how it feels with Charles. My family, my life with Victor, all the demands and expectations of family life feel like those branches tearing at my body, and though I move as quickly as I can, I am always trapped inside them. But Charles – Charles is the secret meadow, fragrant with sweet grass, where I lie for as long as I dare, and when I rise, I am renewed enough to enter my life again.

It is not a friendship. That lie was the first to go.

He keeps me alive. I fear myself without him.

Charles, like Victor, likes talk. He constantly wants to recite poetry, to compare me to a flower or fruit, or a hillside at dusk. I couldn't care less about the words or the romance. I've had enough of fancy language. I don't want language at all, in fact. I want the slap of bodies in the act of love. I want the salt muscle of a kiss.

Charles likes to talk, but with Charlotte I can have my way. She is not so interested in words. Often she seems bewildered by being Charlotte, and has to concentrate on the business of a woman – holding her skirts, walking with dainty steps – all of which, thankfully, takes away her desire to compare me to a rose bush.

Charlotte yields to me, and the pleasure in this is exquisite, addictive. I have never felt such power and I am greedy for it. The moment she leaves my side, I long for her return.

But I wish that I believed my lies, because I cannot reconcile my desire for my lover with the fact that I have become an adultress.

When Charlotte and I meet in the church, we arrive and depart separately. I always ask her to leave first, and I sit there in the pew until I can no longer hear her tentative footsteps on the stone. Then I get down on my knees and pray for a forgiveness I don't deserve.

~ ~ ~ ~ ~

My husband and I were childhood sweethearts. This was back when I believed that the love poems he wrote me were about me, rather than about his need to write them.

I believed the poetry. I believed the kisses. I believed the sloppy eagerness of my own heart. We married, and for a while I was the happiest I've ever been. But when the children came and I, necessarily, turned my attentions to them, Victor felt rebuffed and disappeared into his work – a work that could absorb all of him if he let it.

That's the simple explanation. But really, it's another lie.

I lost my desire for Victor. I found his kisses repulsive, and his constant need to be in my bed was not my need.

But I am married to him. I have a duty and a contract, and nothing justifies the betrayal of my wedding vows. It doesn't matter that I have lost my desire for my husband. This is the natural state of any marriage and I should just accept it. Why can't I just accept it?

When I'm down on my knees in the church, worrying a line of prayer from my lips, I feel disgust for my actions, and a desperation to remedy them. But I never feel that God hears me or understands. I never know what to do to absolve my sins. I just rise and go back to my family.

Each time I meet with Charles, my situation becomes more intolerable, and I become more miserable because of it.

As a girl I ran after my sister through the woods. I climbed trees. I made a lance out of a sapling and speared a grouse. I was as tall and strong as any boy. This is what Victor and I had in common when we were young, a longing to express ourselves physically, a need to be active and in the world.

I am still that same being, and it is clear to me that I must do something about my situation. God is not going to help me. Charles cannot do anything. He has asked me to leave my marriage. That is the most he can do. The choice is mine to make. I must leave Charles, or I must leave Victor.

There is no point in lying to myself any more.

But to leave Victor, I will probably have to leave my children, because how could I afford to support them? My sister is sympathetic, and she might take us in for a while, but I have four children. She will not be able to house us for long. And really, how can I leave my children? How will God forgive that sin? Demanding as they sometimes are, I love them absolutely.

Most nights, after my little ones are in bed, I walk through each of their rooms, watching them sleep. They are all so beautiful. And when one of them has a dream and twitches or cries out, I run to comfort him without thinking, as I run to comfort them through every day. It is impossible to imagine not being attached to them, not being available to respond to their every need.

But I do imagine this. I lie in my bed after I have visited my children's rooms. Victor likes to work late, is always working late, and so I lie in my bed alone, imagining Charles there beside me. There could be no sweeter pleasure than waking up with him every morning, than turning over in the night to touch his soft skin.

So, slowly, over time, I make myself believe the impossible. In order to be with my lover, I have to abandon my children.

I tell myself that they are my husband's children as well. He has formed a special bond with Léopoldine, and Charles and François-Victor will learn to be men from him. They need to remain with him. I could leave them in his care and he would look after them. He does love them.

So, that is what I will do. I will take my baby, Dédé, with me, and I will leave the older children with their father. One child I can manage. One child I can bring with me to Charles.

Dédé is much too young to abandon. She still has such need of me. The others are more independent and they become more independent with every day.

I make this decision, and I tell no one about it. Not Charles. Not even Julie. It sickens me to think that this is what I will do, but I know that I will do it, just as I plunged the sharpened stick into the breast of the grouse. Feeling badly about it didn't stop me from killing the bird. I have the sort of courage that a soldier has, and mostly it is useless to me. I would be good in a duel, better than Charles, who is constantly being challenged, but of course no woman is ever required to fight a duel. No, my courage will never be offered up to heroics, but only to the reprehensible act of forsaking my children.

I make my decision, and I await my opportunity to act, and, as it turns out, I do not have to wait long.

Victor comes home one evening and announces that we are moving. The landlord is evicting us because of all the controversy surrounding *Hernani*.

"I've found us an apartment," says Victor after supper. "On rue Jean-Goujon. It's very spacious and bright. You'll love it."

"That's the other side of the river."

"I have to be near the theatre. Now more than ever. It's very important. You know that."

Victor is always telling me what I know. Once I used to argue with him about this, but now I can't be bothered. He's clearly made up his mind. The apartment is already rented. He has had packing cases delivered and has told the children that we're moving.

It will be very difficult to rendezvous with Charles if we live across the river. It's difficult now, when we live two doors apart.

"When?" I say.

"The beginning of the month."

That's in just over a week.

"Why didn't you tell me before this?"

"It happened so quickly. I didn't know before this."

We are standing by the window in the sitting room, the window that overlooks the garden. Outside the children are playing some game that involves racing at top speed around the pond. It is time to call them in for bed, which is why I went over to the window in the first place.

Victor is standing beside me. He's not looking out into the garden, but rather is staring down at his hands resting on the window ledge. I look down as well. His hands are broad, ink-stained, the nails chipped and dirty. These hands write the words that keep us all alive. They are also the hands that wrote the play that is forcing us to move across the river.

Victor slides his right hand towards my left hand, tentatively, like a cat slinking up on a bird.

"It will be an adventure, my darling," he says.

I turn from the window before he can touch me.

"I must call the children in for bed."

I sit on the edge of Dédé's bed after she is tucked in and ready for sleep. She is excited about the move, keeps wanting to ask me questions, to talk about it.

"Will there be flowers over there?" she asks. "Will there be cats?"

"It's the other side of the river, not the other side of the world," I say.

"Will there be apples?"

"Of course."

"Will I have a bed?"

"You will have this bed. We will load it into a cart and it will travel across the river and be set down in your new room."

Dédé laughs delightedly and clutches my hand. "Can I lie in it when it is on the cart?" she asks.

"Shall we pretend?" I say. "Move over." I slide down beside her on the narrow bed and she rolls into my arms. "There would be stars above us. Bright stars. Close your eyes and tell me when you see them."

Dédé squirms in my arms. "I see them! I see them!"

"And the cart would be bumpy over the cobblestones." I gently rock her in my arms, back and forth, back and forth. "The night air might be chill, but you would be tucked up so warm in your bed." I tighten my arms around her. "You would be so safe and warm." I continue to rock my daughter, closing my eyes as well, imagining the sharp stars above us, and the dank smell of the river; the yellow lick of lamplight on the bridges.

Dédé's breath opens into sleep, but I stay with her on the bed, keep her in my arms. She is so light and small, more like a bird than a child. My little one. My treasure.

I am a selfish woman to want more than my children. It should be enough to care for them, to love them like this. For every other woman it would be enough. Why isn't it enough for me?

I open my jewellery box and shove its contents into a carpet bag. I put the letters from Charles in there as well, and some of the gifts my children have given me – drawings, a swan feather, dried flowers. I take the pencil portraits I have made of the children, and some of the first poems that Victor wrote to me, when we were newly in love.

I will send for my dresses. I will send for my cloaks. I will send for the carpets and tapestries that belonged to my family. I will send for the few sticks of furniture that are my own. I will send for my books and paintings.

Downstairs Victor packs for the family. I can hear him crashing things into the packing crates. Upstairs I take only what I can't bear to be parted from tonight, for I have made up my mind that I will leave after Victor has gone to bed. I will carry Dédé from her slumber and we will walk the short distance to Charles's house. She has fallen asleep on the story of moving, and she will wake to find that it is true, although it will not be the move she had imagined. Still, I will make sure that there are flowers and apples and cats for her in her new life.

I will send for her bed.

I don't hear the door, but I do hear the voices. Victor's booming voice, and then the fainter, more feminine voice of Charles. I stiffen, and my breath comes fast and shallow. I can't hear what they're saying, so I drop the carpet bag on my bed and creep from my bedroom into the hallway. I move slowly down the corridor, my feet finding the boards that don't creak, until I am standing near the top of the stairs. From this spot I can hear everything perfectly.

At first I think that they are talking about the play, because this is what they often talk about, Victor is always enlisting Charles to give an opinion on his writing. But I realize quite quickly that they are not discussing literature. No, Charles is telling Victor that he and I are having an affair.

My legs buckle. I lean against the wall. I can't believe he is doing this. Why is he doing this?

The voices float up to me, as though Charles and Victor are in a play and I am sitting in the balcony, having paid handsomely for a ticket to this theatre.

Charles is boasting. Victor is scornful. Charles offers proof. Victor is confused and bewildered. Charles is penitent. Victor is outraged. Charles tries to take back what he has said. Victor won't let him.

It has all the heightened emotion of any good drama, all the elements of a drama that Victor might have written himself.

~~~~~

I remember the first time I met Charles. He came to visit Victor and me on rue de Vaugirard, when we lived above a joiner's shop. Victor had invited him round, was ecstatic about his visit because Charles had given Victor's poems a wonderful review in the *Globe*. Victor felt that he'd found a champion in the press, someone to review his work favourably and advance his reputation. He practically threw himself down the stairs when he heard the knock at the apartment door.

I don't remember what we ate, or the time of year, or whether I was pregnant yet with my first child. I don't remember where we sat, whether there was a fire, if there was rain at the window, what I was wearing, how much wine we drank. It is strange how the details can fall away and yet the feelings remain.

I had two feelings that night. The first was one of relief. If Victor had a friend that he could talk poetry to, then he would have no need to be constantly discussing it with me. I had initially been flattered that he valued my opinion so highly, but then I saw him have the same discussions with his friends, with my sister's husband, with the fishmonger and the lamplighter. It was a discussion he was having with himself, except that it helped Victor to be able to have his inner conversations out loud. I, like all his other listeners, was required to hear his ideas, not to comment upon them. And if there was someone else willing to take my place in this, so much the better.

Later, Charles remarked on my silence during that first evening, how I had said not a word to him when he came for supper. It was not that I intended to be rude, or uninterested in his company, but rather that I was so grateful he was engaging Victor in conversation, that I feared anything I said would snap that thread. For the first time since we had married, I could have my own thoughts, and not have to be reacting to Victor's. I could sit over my needlework and muddle through my feelings,

think about the events of the day, or of my life so far, anticipate the pleasures of the evening, when, after our guest had
departed, my husband would take me to bed.

I had nothing *but* desire for Victor in those days.

The second feeling I remember having that night was
curiosity. Who was this young man who wanted so badly to
make a friend of my husband? I watched him out of the corner
of my eye. He looked a little like a bird, with his hooked nose
and high forehead – like a bird of prey. And, like a bird of prey,
he was intent on his target. He wanted Victor to like him. He
fawned and fussed, laughed a beat after my husband started
laughing, repeated the same words back to Victor, a few minutes
after Victor had said them. How agreeable he was being! How
friendly!

What did he want?

I asked Charles this once, when we were lying in bed in our
hotel room, limbs entwined. Be honest, I said, because I felt that
around his own ambitions, he was not always truthful.

I believed him a genius, he said. *I wanted him to help me become
a better poet.*

But this was not all. The feeling I had that first night was
a feeling I sometimes had later on, once Charles and I were
lovers. It was faint then, came to me like a whiff of stale perfume
carried by the breeze.

What I felt that night was that Charles did not just want to
please Victor, but rather that he wanted to *be* Victor.

Had I just exchanged one man for a lesser version of the
same man? Was I merely a trophy to be flourished and fought
over in this contest between Charles and Victor? Was everything really about literature after all?

This is partly why I prefer Charlotte. She would not confess
our affair to Victor. She would keep it secret. She would keep
it sacred.

~ ~ ~ ~ ~

The shouting has subsided. The voices are quieter. There is the clink of glasses. Now Charles and Victor are talking. They are drinking wine.

I walk back along the hallway towards my bedroom, not caring if they hear the creaking floor. I push open the door, sit down heavily on the edge of my bed. There is the carpet bag with its precious sentimental cargo – all that hopefulness I felt, mere moments ago.

Would life with Charles really be different from life with Victor?

I put my head in my hands and weep.

By the time I hear his heavy tread on the stairs, I have stopped crying. When he steps through my bedroom door, I am sitting up straight, composed, my hands folded demurely in my lap.

Victor has had all his emotion with Charles. They have fought and talked and drunk wine, like lovers in a spat. By the time he comes to me, he is spent. He stands there in the doorway, a shadow framed by shadow.

"You will end this," he says. "I will not be shamed by your behaviour for one more instant."

He doesn't wait for my reply, or even for my acknowledgement that I know what he is talking about. It is not a discussion. He takes it for granted that I have been eavesdropping. He turns and walks back down the hallway, back down the stairs. In a few moments I can hear the noises of his resumed packing.

Once, when I was running towards Charles at the Luxembourg Gardens, he grabbed me, in full flight, before I collided with him, and he asked me if I was running towards him, or simply fleeing Victor. Perhaps it was both.

When I was a girl, I had the ambitions of a boy. I could run and jump and ride a horse. I was good at drawing, and good at writing. When I fell in love with Victor, I attached my ambitions to his own, craved his successes, wished for him to be a great artist. My own desires fell away when we married, when I became pregnant, when I had my four sweet children.

I didn't think they would ever come back.

But somehow my ambitions have returned as a single drive, as the force that compels me to love Charles and Charlotte and not Victor.

When I rush towards Charles along the gravel path of the Jardin du Luxembourg, just as I ran out into the meadow as a girl, chasing after my sister through the long grass, I am not in flight. I am hurtling headlong, with no way to stop the momentum I've gathered.

And what I want, what I long for, is not to escape so much as simply to arrive.

CHARLES

THE HUGOS HAVE MOVED. I have not seen my beloved in weeks. Despite Victor's orders that I end my affair with his wife, I have no intention of doing so. The brief notes that Adèle has managed to send me reassure me that she has no plan to end the affair either. But we have encountered great difficulty in seeing one another of late. Victor does not leave Adèle alone for a moment. I have had to write secret letters to her and leave them, under the name Madame Simon, at the Poste Restante. She has sent letters to me by foot messenger, often using the same dim-witted girl who used to board with the Hugos. And despite his avowal that our friendship would not be affected by my love for his wife, Victor always treats me awkwardly when we meet. Thankfully, this is not often, as he has been kept busy with his change of residence and his new book about Cathédrale Notre-Dame.

In the absence of my beloved Adèle, I write poems for her. I want to document our love. I don't want to forget a moment of it – not a word, not a touch. The book is to be called *Livre d'amour*, and I have used real names, transcribed things that Adèle has said, noted our meetings in the church and named the hotel, the Saint-Paul, where we rendezvous for sex. I have disguised nothing. It is my heart laid bare.

But I will never have the volume printed, so I am safe to confess anything I want. The pages are my companion. The words carry my memory of love. They are for me, and for me alone – although I might be persuaded to show some of the poems to Adèle, if she insists.

It is a tragedy that this secret book contains my best work. I have always wanted to be a great poet, and here I must admit that I think Victor is a great poet. It is only his plays that I object to so strenuously. But his verse is beautiful.

Still, *Livre d'amour* is a good book. I know it is. *It is my life, in love and stagnant. /An absence of pleasure, on a base of happiness.* And it is Adèle's life. I have complete freedom to do as I please. I not only tell our secrets, mine and Adèle's, but I tell *her* secrets. Stories of her youth, and stories of her marriage to the "dark husband". I write hoping "that you will always be this Adèle whom I love". I write of "our short joy/our long delay". Sometimes the poems seem as real as though I am living the moments again. *It is the hour when you should be taken back. Here, give me your hand. Let us pretend we have tomorrow.*

I talk about each time we have met, what happened, what was said. I have even written a poem to little Adèle, young Dédé. Since she is so small, she is often the one child who will accompany us on our walks through the orchard. There is no chance that she will relay anything of our meetings back to Victor, and the fact that she is my godchild means that I am more fond of her than I am of Adèle's other children.

Delicious child that her mother sends to me, /Last born child of the husband whose joy I broke; /Her face lit up by twenty moons.

More than once Adèle and I, lost in our passion, have neglected the cries of the child.

Your mother and I are burning meteors. /So many storms have passed since your innocent hour. /We cannot be the shelter you need.

I have ended this poem with a direct address to little Adèle, to a time when she is old enough to read and understand my words because, even though I am showing my book to no one, perhaps I will give this one poem to my godchild. It is not just that she is my godchild that makes me so fond of the girl. She has her mother's name. She was born shortly before our love began, so she has grown with that love. I like her nature and I feel that it resembles mine. Sometimes I even entertain the fantasy that she is our child.

Once, when we were all sitting in the garden and Adèle was afraid that Victor would come out to join us at any moment, she was holding little Adèle tightly on her lap when what she really wanted was to embrace me. The little girl cried out, "Mother, why do you love me so much today?" as though she knew, as though she felt what her mother was really feeling.

Love your mother, child – but here is the bitter thing. / The fire which we crave also devours us.

I am fond of particular lines, particular images. I have described the bat as *the swallow of the night*. I have said, *When wisdom is painful, it is wiser to be unaware.* And I have returned again and again to the lovers, to Adèle and me – comparing us to Orpheo and Eurydice, lamenting our separation, rejoicing in our union.

Other lovers had, in their walk, more flowered paths, the happier trance. / And made around them, better singers of the birds.

It makes sense that my great love would yield a great work. How could it be otherwise? It would be an insult to Adèle to write mediocre poems about her, to find her only mildly inspiring as a muse. I am a writer. The proof of how I am feeling is always in my pen.

I sit in my room, late into the night, with sheaves of paper and pots of ink. The drips from the guttering candle seal my words with wax. The breeze blows in from the open window and ruffles the pages. I think of my love, streets away now, and I write to bring her close again. Words are the rope with which I haul memory back.

Doesn't everyone have a book of love to write? I look up from my desk and see, through the crack in the drapes, the flickering candlelight in the houses across the way. What if each of those people in each of those rooms is engaged in the writing of a *Livre d'amour*?

And then another thought occurs to me. What if my book of love is just too good to keep private?

ADÈLE MEETS ME in the Jardin du Luxembourg. She has Dédé with her, is dragging the girl along the path to where I wait for them on a chair in the shade. If I was another kind of man I might leap up when I see her hurrying through the grove of trees, rush out to meet her. But it is one of my great pleasures to watch my lover come towards me, and so I sit and relish the full moment, listen to the scuff of her feet on the gravel path, the birdsong in the air around her.

We don't embrace. She flops onto the chair beside mine, letting go of Dédé's hand. The girl slumps down onto the dusty ground.

"I can't stay long," says Adèle. "Victor is watching my every move. He might even have followed me here." She scans the avenue of trees anxiously, and I do the same, fully expecting to see the compact figure of Victor Hugo crouching there.

"I'm so sorry," I say. "Telling Victor of the affair is perhaps the stupidest thing I have ever done."

"I don't blame you," says Adèle, and I think (not for the first time) how she is a much better person than I am. If the situation had been reversed, I would definitely have blamed her.

"I don't blame you," she continues. "It just makes every-thing more difficult."

"But if I hadn't told him?"

"The fact of Victor would remain," says Adèle. "Whether he knows about us or not, he's still an impediment to our happiness."

"He insisted we would remain friends."

"He calls you a twisty little cheat."

I look down at Dédé. She's playing in the dirt by our feet with a stick and a beetle.

"Come away with me."

"Where to? You have no money. I have no money. And then there's the question of the children." Adèle also looks down at her daughter, and Dédé, feeling our gazes upon her, looks up and smiles at us both.

"And besides," says Adèle, "Victor is making plans for us to go away."

"Where?" That shrewd versifier. It is a pre-emptive move to take his family on a holiday.

"Some friend has a château in Bièvres and he has made arrangements for us to go there for the rest of the summer."

Bièvres is not that far away from the city. It is a small town about an hour south of Paris. But it is small, and if I followed the family there I would be noticed.

The rest of the summer is a very long time.

"Well, I will go away too," I say. "To Belgium." It's the first place that comes into my head, and the truth is that I can ill afford to go anywhere at the moment. I must remain chained to my desk at the *Globe*, writing my reviews.

Adèle squeezes my thigh. "I love it when you're petulant," she says. "You get such a haughty look."

I reach across and squeeze *her* thigh and feel, through my fingertips, the shock of desire beginning its crawl along my nerves.

"Damn him," I say.

"I'll write to you in Belgium," says Adèle. "I should be able to manage that."

Now, because I mentioned it in a moment's rashness, I'm actually going to have to travel to Belgium. Why do I do these things? Why can't I be stopped?

"I'll leave word of where I am at the Poste Restante in Bièvres," I say, resigned to my ridiculous fate. I suppose I can convince the *Globe* editor to let me do my reviews from some cheap hotel in Brussels for a week or so.

"Has Victor finished his book about Notre-Dame then?" I ask.

"What?"

"Well, he wouldn't be prepared to travel away from his working routine if he was still writing that book."

"Yes, he's moved on to thinking about a new play." Adèle looks away from me, but I have seen the shadow of something cross her face. Victor must have told her that they were to make a change of residence because he wanted to revive their marriage, not because he had just finished a book and was waiting to fill up with inspiration for the next one. Victor must have told Adèle this, and Adèle must have actually believed him.

MY HOTEL ROOM IN BRUSSELS is horrid. It is cramped and has bed bugs. The view from the window is down into an alley. I sit in the room all day, trying to pen my wretched reviews, and in the evenings I slouch along the streets looking for an inexpensive place to dine. The only thing that keeps me from utter desolation are the letters that Adèle writes to me from Bièvres. They are letters of reassurance, proclaiming her love for me, telling me what a bore Victor is being. But I only half believe her. A small worm of doubt has wriggled its way into our love.

I lie on the hotel room bed, with its litter of books and papers, and read Adèle's letters over and over, looking for a word out of place, a word that can be pried loose and which will let down an avalanche of betrayal.

But I don't find this, and after a few days of re-reading the letters, I relax and trust again that all is well between us.

And then I receive another letter, not one from Adèle, but from Monsieur Hugo himself. I don't like to think how he has found my address – discovering his wife's letters to me, or forcing her to confess – and I slit open the envelope with great trepidation.

Victor writes to me in a mood of bonhomie that reads as false. I skip over the first few sentences, the friendly greeting and enquiry into my health and well-being. I skip down to the second paragraph. In my experience, what someone really wants to say is never in the beginning of a letter. It is in the second or third paragraph.

And there it is, in Victor's second paragraph, where he boasts that Adèle is doing well, that he has never known her to be so happy, that it was such a good idea for them to get away together. He writes that Adèle seems positively radiant with happiness.

This is more than I can bear. I throw open my trunk and begin to toss in my clothes and books.

After a brief stop in Paris to rid myself of certain belongings, and pick up other items, I take a coach south to Bièvres. It is easy to find accommodation in a local inn, and easy to find the château where Adèle and Victor are staying. Everyone knows the famous author.

The château is surrounded by a forest, and for the first day I flit like a bird through the trees on the edge of this forest, hoping to catch a glimpse of Adèle leaving the grounds. But this proves futile, and really the forest is just a little too distant from the château to get a good look without a spyglass, so I change my plan.

I change my clothes, and go as Charlotte to the local church. I know my Adèle. It will only be a matter of time before she feels a need to pray or confess.

I go to the church and I sit in a pew at the back, and I wait.

On the third day, the doors open and I watch as Adèle walks up the aisle of the church. Because she isn't expecting me, she isn't looking for me, and she walks right past me to sit in a pew several rows up. I wait until she has her head bowed in prayer and then I slip out of where I am and move up to her pew. She raises her head when I enter the row and immediately knows who I am.

"Charlotte. My love." Her face lights up. She is, as her husband said in his boastful letter, positively radiant with happiness. All my doubts evaporate. She has not returned her heart to Victor. She is still mine.

~ ~ ~ ~ ~

We meet in the church. We meet in the forest. I lurk among the trees like a madman. We kiss in the choir loft. I fondle her by a waterfall. She takes flowers home to press with the children. She runs back to the château with twigs in her hair and grass stains on her dress.

We are being foolish and we know it.

"It is only a matter of time," says Adèle, at the end of the first week, "before Victor finds us out."

We are lying in the forest in the middle of a gorse bush where I have hollowed us out a lair. It is how I spent my morning while waiting for Adèle to leave the château. I fear I am going feral. We are living like rabbits.

"What can we do?" I am trying to untie her stays but I keep getting poked by sticks. "These are desperate times." The need to keep our love even more secret has intensified the passion. I run my hand up the inside of her thigh. She shivers in delight.

"I have never been happier," I exclaim. "I want to live like this forever."

"In the shrubbery?"

"No." I bend to kiss her. "Like this. With you. Near you."

Adèle struggles up onto her elbows. "Charles," she says. "I don't want to get caught. You have to go back to Paris."

I feel as though I have been run through with a sabre, as though the ground beneath Adèle and me is already soaked with my blood.

"You can't mean that."

"But, I do. I do." Adèle strokes my cheek. "My treasure," she says. "I just can't risk it."

"But weren't you hoping that I might arrive?"

"Yes, I was."

"And how will it be when I leave?"

Adèle sighs, lowers herself back down on to the dirt.

"Unbearable," she says, as she pulls me down on top of her. "I would die without you."

I have been turned out of the inn where I was staying because the proprietress thought I was bringing prostitutes there. I was careless one afternoon and returned to the inn still dressed as Charlotte. This woman shamelessly went up to my room and entered and presumably pleasured me, and now I have been thrown out of my lodgings.

When I go to another inn, seeking accommodation, the innkeeper looks at my name as I sign the register.

"We're full up," he says.

"But you just told me I could have a room."

He snatches the register away from me. "I lied."

"Why would you do that?"

He shrugs. "I don't want you here."

Bièvres is a small place. The townspeople probably know about Adèle and me, and view our love as scandalous. Even this lowly innkeeper thinks I am an enemy of decency. I should challenge him to a duel for his insolence, but I can't be bothered and I pick up my bags.

It is time to go back to Paris, back to my love poems.

WHILE I WAIT FOR ADÈLE to return from the country, I have taken to coming to Cathédrale Notre-Dame every evening after supper. Not to the church where I usually meet my lover, but to *the* church, the great cathedral, the heart of the city.

I have read Victor's book, and I have to admit I liked it. I did wonder briefly if the horribly disfigured hunchback who lives in the bell tower, Quasimodo, was modelled on me, but mostly I've been impressed by the beautiful descriptions of the church, by Victor's intent to raise the public's awareness of the building's neglect. It was damaged during the first revolution and badly needs repair. Victor's story is set in the church, but the church is really the main character. I admire my old friend's desire to save such a monumental part of Paris's history. It is a noble gesture.

And the book is selling very well.

It is not far to walk from my house to where the church rests on the Ile de la Cité, the small island in the middle of the Seine that used to be the entire city of Paris. Now, that island is anchored to the city proper by five bridges, like ropes mooring a ship to the shore.

The summer evenings are long and there is still considerable light outside when I enter the building during the last mass of the day. If it is crowded, I sit in a pew near the back, under the vaulted ceiling, made, as all church ceilings were made, to imitate the vastness of the heavens.

An entire army could march through the arches and they

would still seem diminutive in relation to the church. Victor is right. It is too grand, too important to fall into decay. The broken statuary deserves to be repaired. The ruined pavement outside needs replacing. I wish I'd thought of writing a book about Notre-Dame myself. But I don't have the same sentimental touch as Victor. I cannot move the masses to action, sound the right romantic chord in people's hearts. My prose is drier. My poetry is too specific.

Notre-Dame and the River Seine, Paris, c. 1865

I sit in the belly of the cathedral and imagine Victor coming here every night after a fevered day's writing. I envy him that experience of holy purpose. He would have walked along the aisles feeling entirely supported in the writing of his book − supported by the church itself. He would have felt chosen. He would have felt blessed. I am more of a believer than Victor, but God loves Victor for helping Notre-Dame, and God hates me for loving Victor's wife.

Religion has its images and codes – arches are hands clasped in prayer, the lily is the flower of the Virgin Mary, the peacock apparently does not decay when it dies and so symbolizes immortality and the resurrection. Every part of every church is like a page in a book. It can be read. Some evenings this is all I do, select a particular piece of wall or window and try to remember what everything means, try to read the interior of the cathedral.

The columns inside Notre-Dame have leaves carved into the stone at the top. They are meant to resemble trees, to remember trees, to remember that the first churches would have been in the forest.

When I sit at the back, the church is long and narrow ahead of me. Sometimes I look straight along it, to the curve of stained glass behind the altar. Sometimes I gaze down at the black and white tiled floor, or up at the high, vaulted ceiling.

In the centre of the ceiling is a round painting of the Madonna and child encircled in a gold frame. The painting is dark and there are gold stars decorating the ceiling around it. From where I sit at the back of the church the medallion looks like a porthole in the ceiling.

This church took two hundred years to build. I marvel at that, how a man could pass four full lifetimes and never see the finished structure.

I enter the cathedral while there is still light in the sky, and I leave when it is dark, when the candles have been lit inside the church and the lamps have been lit on the bridges outside. I move from one world back to another.

At first when I go to Notre-Dame I think of Victor and his

book. Then I think of how I would wait for Adèle in our little church, how impatient I would be for her to arrive, to see her. But after the third or fourth night of coming to the cathedral after supper I realize that I am coming for myself, that I am not imitating anyone, or waiting for anyone. I have entered this building not to worship another, but rather to please myself.

I HAVE DECIDED TO MOVE IN with my mother on the rue du Montparnasse. It is a small house and I will have to make do with less privacy, but it will be a saving for me to throw in my lot, temporarily, with Madame Sainte-Beuve. My income is dependent on work that comes my way, and when there isn't much of this I cannot eat or pay my rent. Now that I am embarked on serious literary pursuits, it seems prudent to save money where I can.

I am fond of Mother, but she is tiresome. We share an emotional sympathy, but she is not much good as an intellectual companion, as I said. Her thoughts are not concerned with symbols and philosophical argument. They are, most likely, dwelling on some lowly gossip she heard on the street that morning, or engaged in the never-ending quest to find her sewing basket, or her spectacles. Sharing a house with her will be more frustrating than rewarding, but it will also mean that I will not have to work so hard at the *Globe*.

Life with Mother is not easy. The first night we are together under one roof again I am sitting up in my new bedroom reading, when I hear the most appalling sounds coming from Mother's bedroom at the end of the corridor. Scraping and scratching, the noise of the floorboards being scored as something heavy is pushed over them.

I wait for the noise to stop. It does not. I put my book aside and go and knock on Mother's bedroom door.

"Are you all right?" I ask.

"Perfectly well, Sainte-Beuve," comes her reply from the other side of the door.

"Why are you moving furniture so late at night?"

"I am not moving furniture."

"But I heard you." Those sounds could not be anything else. I turn the doorknob, but the door won't open more than a fraction. "Mother, let me in."

"I'm afraid I cannot, Sainte-Beuve," says Mother through the closed door. "You see, I'm barricaded in for the night."

"Whatever for?"

"So that thieves may not enter my bedchamber and have done with me."

Mother is afraid of being robbed and murdered. She is afraid of slipping on the cobblestones when it rains. She is afraid to ride in a cab pulled by a black horse, to open her front door at night, to walk in unfamiliar streets. I do not know when she suddenly became so nervous of life. She seemed so robust when I was young.

"Don't be foolish," I say to her at least once a day, but she is quick to point out that it is her house and she will conduct herself there exactly as she pleases. And I have no rebuttal for that.

Adèle has returned to Paris, but I have not seen her. I sent word to her under her alias at the Poste Restante to let her know that I have moved, but I have had no word back from her to say when we might meet. I am trying not to despair. I am trying to concentrate on the business of moving house and writing my poems. I must put Adèle out of my mind, for to think of her causes me to miss her, and when I miss her I am incapable of getting anything done.

The Hugos have moved again. All of Paris knows this, knows how famous Victor has become, how well his book about Notre-Dame has sold, not only in France, but all over the world. The household has left rue Jean-Goujon for Place Royale, where, apparently, they have a magnificent apartment in the Hôtel de Rohan-Guémené.

Love, increasingly, seems more of an affliction than a blessing.

And now, a ridiculous thing has happened. I have been called up to serve in the Garde nationale. I should explain that the Garde is a militia made up of the middle class. When one is summoned to the Garde nationale, he is given a blue uniform and a rifle and is expected to help keep peace in the streets, stop the vandalism and thieving that seems so much a part of city life.

The idea of the rifle and the uniform is tempting, but after having made the great sacrifice of moving in with my mother to conserve time and money, I just cannot afford to add yet another duty to my busy life. I will never get my poems written if I do not give them my full attention. So I have ignored the summons and now I have been charged with neglecting my civic duty and have been condemned, in absentia, to serve a prison sentence for this offence.

I have gone into hiding. Under the name Charles Delorme, I have rented cheap rooms at the Hôtel de Rouen. The hotel is on the right bank of the river, in the Cour du Commerce, a twisting series of alleys that holds all manner of shops and services. If I am chased into the Cour du Commerce, there are many places to hide. And if I am chased into the Hôtel de Rouen, there are four exits by which I can escape, one door to the south, one to the north, one to the east, and one to the west.

My rooms are on the third floor and look out over the distant Jardin du Luxembourg, out over those perfect days not long ago when I walked through the orchard with Adèle, fully believing that our love was strong enough to bear our circumstances.

I am less convinced now. As I said, she sends no word to me, no reassurance of her love, no promise of meeting.

My two rooms cost only twenty-three francs a month, with morning coffee included. The staircase to the third floor is as steep as a ladder. The hallway is dark and narrow. But when I throw open the door to the small room where I am to write, I feel only liberation at my prospects. The proprietors of the hotel, Monsieur and Madame Ladame, are friendly and courteous. They can be relied upon to warn me if the police should arrive to arrest me.

My mother, however, is unhappy with my arrangement. She was all in favour of my spending time in the Garde nationale. She thought it would be good for my character and for my figure, which has grown a little plumper of late. According to her, the Hôtel de Rouen is not a suitable place for a gentleman. I pronounce the name as *Hôtel de Rohan*, to make it sound more noble, to echo Victor's prestigious new lodgings, but she is not convinced. She is disappointed in me, in my choices. "I would rather have given birth to a freemason," she says.

I will spend eight years in these hotel rooms, but I don't know that yet, of course. Now, in my thirtieth year, I climb the stairs, puffing my way along the hallway to the rooms numbered nineteen and twenty. One small space in which to sleep. One small space in which to work. I have successfully eluded both the Garde nationale and the police. My mother knows where I am and, even though she disapproves of me at the moment, she will not turn me in. What I know now, when I open the door of the room I will work in, is that I have a desk by a window, and a view out over the Jardin du Luxembourg, out to the fields that lie beyond the orchard. I have ink and paper and ideas. I have left Charles Sainte-Beuve behind. I am now Charles Delorme. I am a free man. And I am a writer.

IT IS THE SILENCE that carries the music.

It is these long days and nights, hunched over the small desk in my room at the Hôtel de Rouen, that will make my name.

I have decided to try my hand at a novel. If Victor can do it, surely I can too. My poems are going well, but I need something more than verse to tell the story of Adèle and me. I need to create a world to live in with her. If I cannot live with her in this world, then I will make an imagined shelter for our love.

But it is harder than I thought, and first I must change some of the identifying details. It is all very well to write my book of love poems for myself, but I desire to be a serious writer and I should try to get this novel published. So I must take liberties to disguise the story of my love.

I decide to set the tale in the time of the Napoleonic campaigns in the 1790s. My hero (me) shall be a soldier in these campaigns. He will be in love with his friend's wife, a Madame de Couaen, and the bulk of the story shall be a testimony to that love.

Well, that certainly sounded good when I thought it up. But writing it down is another matter. The plot falls away quite quickly, as overcooked meat slips from the bone, and the book becomes not so much an exploration of my love for Adèle as the exposure of it. After a day's work I feel raw and trembling, barely have the strength to stumble down the staircase in search of supper. And on the way back up I must grasp the large brass ball on the landing railing with both my hands to steady myself before proceeding down the hallway, back to my room and the torture that this writing has become.

I thought there would be peace in the enterprise, but writing the story down just lays it bare again. Writing of Adèle does not offer me any rest. It just makes me miss her more acutely. It just makes me relive all of our moments together and ache for those moments to be repeated.

I must be free of this torment. I must kill off Madame de Couaen.

What I do like are the rituals: the morning shave in room number twenty, the coffee delivered by Madame Ladame. I like the sound of the stairs creaking as she climbs slowly up with cup in hand. I drink the coffee. I look out the window. I pace around the room, working myself into a state of restless agitation, that I now recognize as the creative state. Then I march next door to room number nineteen, stride across to the desk and fling myself down wretchedly. My pen lurches over the first few sentences, but then it moves swiftly and fluently. After I have killed off Madame de Couaen, the words are released from me as though they were water flowing from a pump. I cannot keep up with my thoughts. My hand races to pin down what seems desperate to flee. I must make tame what wants to remain wild, although sometimes there is much lost in this translation from feeling to meaning.

But sometimes too I will write something that I didn't realize was true until I'd secured it to the page. I write, "Men's destinies do not correspond to the energy in their souls", and I have to push my chair back from the table while I think about the truth of this. For this is how it is in me. My outward life at the moment is fairly placid, boring even, but my internal life rages with feeling. They are not reconciled, or perhaps even reconcilable. And isn't this also the fate of the writer? To write is the most passive of acts. There is more excitement to be found in observing someone asleep. And yet what surges through the writer's veins while he is writing is thrilling and wild. The more sedate a writer's life appears to be on the outside, the more imaginative he is able to be inside himself, and the more extraordinary work is possible.

My hero (me) is good on horseback. When emotions are too much for him, he simply rides off. Later he rides back. Once he says, in all seriousness, "Can a man keep a flame burning in his breast without his clothes catching fire?"

It is something to consider. My love for Adèle must be visible to all who see us together. In some ways it is a relief to be in exile at the Hôtel de Rouen. I am not in danger of being discovered making love to Adèle in my novel.

When my hand is tired and cramped from writing, or when I must open another bottle of ink or replenish my sheaf of paper, I pause from my work and look out of the window, across the river, out over the countryside that borders the outer edge of the Jardin du Luxembourg. I like this view. I like being so high up, as though I am on the topmast of a ship.

My hero (me) narrates the second part of the book from on board a ship. He has to periodically put down his pen to attend to the duties of sailing.

When I write about our love, I realize how unsettled it has made me. I now depend on my morning ritual of shaving, coffee, pacing, writing. I can lean on it and, on the bad days, the unsteady days, it will hold me up. There was nothing to lean on in my love for Adèle. We did not have the luxury of routine. Every time we met it was fraught with stored-up emotion, with the fear that we would not be able to meet again soon.

My hero (me) goes to the monastery at Port-Royal. He decides to undergo training for the priesthood and spends his days praying, reading, going for long walks, eating simple meals with the monks. His small cell is sparsely furnished and he does not want for more. Occasionally there is singing at a meal. More occasionally there is cake. The time passes blessedly, uneventfully.

After he is ordained, he leaves the monastery, riding off on horseback to visit Madame de Couaen. When he gets to her house he finds her on her deathbed. She is, of course, overjoyed at seeing him, and she asks him, with her husband's blessing, to hear her last confession and deliver her the sacraments. He does this, with great feeling. She is grateful. She dies.

I put down my pen. I feel drained of words, empty of emotion. By killing off Madame de Couaen, I have preserved the love she felt for my hero (me) without having to consider its future. It has met a logical end. The love has transcended itself from a physical plane to a spiritual one, but it has remained constant. I fear there will be nothing so convenient for Adèle and me. Our future is, unfortunately, beyond the control of my pen.

I HAVE MADE A NEW FRIEND.

Even though I am in hiding from the militia, I am still reviewing for the *Globe*. It was my good fortune to be assigned two novels by the same author. Excellent books, both of them, and I say as much in my reviews. I also write to the author, conveying my admiration and asking if I can meet with him.

He agrees, and so I put on a hat to disguise my face, puff up the steep stairs to his apartment, and knock on his door.

"Ah, Sainte-Beuve. Welcome." The door opens to allow me admittance, but I remain in the hallway, confused.

"George?"

"The same."

I almost burst into laughter, but that would be rude, so I restrain myself (barely) and walk into the apartment of the young, brilliant Parisian author.

George Sand is a woman. Despite her masculine pen name, and her male dress, and her cigarette smoking – she is very much a woman. She sports male dress in order to have more freedom in society.

Friendship is best when it is founded on mutual respect, or when there is a sameness of character, and George and I are full of admiration for each other's work. We were also born in the same year. But what binds us most closely together is love, and the torment it offers us.

Once, George, despairing of her many unsatisfactory affairs, asked me, "What is love?"

George Sand

"Tears," I replied. "If you weep, you love."

"I have asked this question of many people," she said. "And you are the only one who has answered honestly."

There are no women allowed in the Hôtel de Rouen, but George Sand, dressed as a man, passes by the inscrutable Madame Ladame without a glance. We sit in room number nineteen and read our novels aloud to each other. Her book, *Leila*, is further along than my *Volupté*, but this does not bother me. She writes faster. Every night, from midnight to dawn, she pens twenty pages. Sometimes, she confesses, she is able to complete a book in as little as thirty days. I admire her industry and her passion. We both believe that one must be moved by what one has written in order for the reader to be moved in turn. Passion is everything.

George's real name is Aurore. As Aurore she was married to a man who was unfaithful and she has left him and her two children. The loss of the children pains her and she hopes to be reunited with them soon, but I am heartened by her example of desertion. Perhaps it could serve as a model for Adèle?

When George and I meet in the Hôtel de Rouen, we always start out by talking about writing, and we always end up by talking about love. One day we are sitting by the open window. It is hot in the room and there is only a tepid breeze to cool us. We have removed our waistcoats. George mops her forehead with a pocket handkerchief.

"Charles," she says, "I need a new lover. My independence is a cage that imprisons me."

I think hard for a moment, running through the tally of writers I know.

"What about Mérimée?" I ask. Prosper Mérimée, the novelist, is a bit of a rake, but he is a strong character, and George's will needs to be matched with a strong character.

"Can you arrange a meeting?"

I have dropped out of Victor's Cénacle, but I am still friends with Mérimée and Emile Deschamps.

"I can."

"Done," says George, as though we have just completed a business transaction.

A week later she is back in my room.

"It was awful," she says. "He was arrogant and a terrible

womanizer. He tired of me and even had the gall to toss me a five franc tip on his way out the door."

"I'm sorry."

"Is there no one else?" George puts her hand on my arm. "I'm fairly desperate, and you're the only one who will help me. I asked Liszt to advise me on love, and he said that the only love worth having was the love of God." George smiles at me, knowing in advance that I will agree with what she is about to say. "But if one has loved a man, it is very hard to love God."

I envy her assurance and her brilliance, and I know that *Leila* will make her famous. It is a wonderful novel. I anticipate a future for her that is full of lovers and full of books. I tell her so.

It strikes me that, if the situation were reversed, she would probably have women to put forth to me as possible lovers. But even the thought of this makes me feel guilty. I still love Adèle, and have told George as much. How could I even think of anyone else? And, more importantly, with my secret, how could anyone think of me? Although I'm half-tempted to ask. What if it was someone very beautiful?

"What about Alfred de Musset?" I ask, ridding myself of treasonous thoughts and getting back to the task at hand. "He's very handsome."

"And very young," says George.

"Full of passion," I say.

That's the magic word, for both of us. George nods her head slowly in agreement, and it is done.

They become lovers practically from their first meeting. She writes to me from Venice, where they have gone together, telling me of their fights, of Alfred's rashness and accusations. He is jealous of her night writing and leaves her to that while he attends violent orgies, returning to her in the mornings full of remorse, then flying into a rage and charging her with wanting to have him committed to an insane asylum.

"I should have known from the beginning," she says, when we see each other again. "I should have known by the names we called each other that the relationship was doomed."

"What were the names?"

"I called him 'my poor child'," George sighs. "It's embarrassing," she says.

"What did he call you?"

"'My big George'."

I'm not sure George will come to me for advice on love again.

Later, George writes to me, "I think right now I am incapable of love, but I am capable of friendship."

I tell George about Charlotte. I tell her about my condition. I have never told anyone other than Adèle, but George is more sympathetic than I would have guessed.

"Poor Charles," she says. "No wonder you mourn the loss of Adèle."

It is a relief to confide in someone, but it does not really change anything fundamental. I still suffer because of my strange body. I still fear that I will never find another lover. And there is a limit to what someone can understand from the outside. I remain as alone as ever inside my skin.

I do remember George in love again, years later. I remember sitting with her and the Polish composer, Frédéric Chopin, in the Jardin du Luxembourg. It is spring. We are sitting on chairs in the sun near the orchard where Adèle and I used to walk so long ago. Frédéric and George are lovers. I have come to meet them, to walk out with them, but as Chopin is sickly and tires easily we have settled on these chairs in the spring sun so he can rest.

For a while we talk, and then we don't, just listen to the wind in the trees overhead. Chopin coughs occasionally, a sharp retort, like a rifle. The wind drags the branches of the trees across the blue patch of sky. The noise is like the sea on the shingle, a noise I remember from my childhood.

My memories, as I write this down, are often out of sequence, out of time. It does not matter to me that events have slipped their chronology. There is a natural order to things, and I am following that now. Recollection is exactly that, a re-collection. And so I have added this later memory of George and Frédéric because it belongs to the group of memories that encompass my friendship with her.

By the time we sat together in the Jardin du Luxembourg George and I had known each other a long time. Our companionship was an easy one. Old friends are as easy with each other as new lovers.

The wind in the trees was the whisper of water on stone. It was the breath of blood in the veins. It was a place where two novelists, George and I, felt perfectly comfortable. A place we had worked hard to get to – in our individual work, and in our friendship. A place entirely without words.

VICTOR HAS A LOVER. She is an actress. Her name is Juliette Drouet and Victor met her when she was playing the part of Princess Negroni in his play, *Lucrèce Borgia*.

I did not get this information from Adèle, whom I still have not seen since I went into hiding, but from George Sand, who says it is the talk of Paris. She tells me that Juliette has become Victor's mistress, and that they are very much in love. No mention of my Adèle and how she must be feeling about this. But I can guess that she will not be happy, and I can hope that this new situation might inspire her to finally leave her husband and be with me.

It is too late to see Juliette Drouet in *Lucrèce Borgia*, but Victor, who is alarmingly prolific these days, has written a new play, *Marie Tudor*, in which his mistress appears with Mademoiselle George, the famous actress, who was once the mistress of Napoleon.

I buy a ticket for opening night.

It is hard not to think of that other night, it seems like ages ago now, when Adèle and I went to see *Hernani* at the same theatre. How excited I was, setting out on that evening's adventure. How my hands shook as I shaved and dressed in anticipation of seeing my beloved.

Now I shave and dress slowly, sluggishly, in my little room at the top of the Hôtel de Rouen. The Hotel of Ruin. There is nothing to hurry my heart along the streets to the Comédie-Française. Nothing to spark my blood as I squeeze along the

Juliette Drouet

row and take my seat in the middle of the first balcony. Adèle
is not beside me, and although I scan the seats in front of me,
and down in the dress circle, I do not see her. Why would she
come to see her husband's mistress on the stage? But I look for
her anyway. It is a force of habit at this point, to look for her,
to hope she is nearby.

Marie Tudor is a play about the British monarchy. There

are only three characters: Queen Mary of England; Lady Jane Grey, who was Queen for just nine days; and the executioner who beheads her. Juliette Drouet plays Lady Jane, and it is clear from the first few moments she is on stage that she is not a good actress. She mumbles her lines and keeps her head bowed, as though she's looking for something she has accidentally dropped on the floor of the stage. It doesn't help her cause that Mademoiselle George, despite being a woman of middle years, is still vibrant and beautiful and is such a magnificent actress. I almost feel sorry for the hapless Juliette. But then I remember Adèle and I take delight in the bad performance, and in the hisses the audience delivers to the young woman.

Victor is in the lobby after the play is over. He is blocking my route to the door and so I slink behind a pillar and wait for him to leave. But he seems intent on talking to the audience as they exit the theatre, scanning the crowd for important people. I can only hide behind the pillar for so long. I am getting looks for my skulking behaviour.

"Charles." He sees me immediately.

"Victor."

He is still compact and sprightly, always looking so ridiculously healthy that I feel like an invalid in comparison.

"What did you think?" he asks.

There is no point in hiding my honesty. There is nothing left of our friendship to protect.

"Lady Jane was dreadful," I say, and I watch as the slightest ripple of pain washes over his face. To someone who didn't know the man it would not even have been noticeable. I admire his professionalism.

"Ah. Well, yes. I think she might be retiring after this performance."

"Won't that affect your relations with her?"

"Not at all, Charles. Not at all." Victor looks almost sorry for me and I hate him in that moment. "How have you been, my old friend? You do not look well. I hear you have been on the run from the Garde nationale."

"I am quite well," I say, but I do not feel that this is entirely true. "And although I am in hiding, my life is otherwise unaffected."

"Really?" Victor regards me quizzically, and I have the sense that he knows Adèle no longer meets with me, that he possesses more information about our affair than I do. "Surely being in hiding would change everything about your life."

It is not a question. Once again, as always in our friendship, Victor has simply pronounced and there is no arguing with his version of reality. And, just as in other times when Victor would disregard my feelings, instead of defending myself, I simply offer up something else for him to savage.

"I'm writing a novel," I say.

"What about?"

"Love."

"That's a very ambitious subject."

We are an island amid the sea of people leaving the theatre and we are buffeted by the departing audience. Victor grabs my shoulder to stop his drift away from me. For a moment we look into each other's eyes, without rancour or pretence or boastfulness. I recognize my old friend, and I see something else in his face. I see his happiness. Juliette Drouet may be a bad actress, but she is undoubtedly a good lover. She has made the great poet very happy.

"Come and see me, Charles," says Victor. "Let us talk more about your novel." For a brief moment it is as it always was between us, as though Victor has forgotten what happened to our friendship, or forgiven it. But then he remembers my trespasses, drops his hand from my shoulder and moves away from me, towards the lobby doors. "Yes," he says, "come and visit us soon. My wife often asks what has become of you."

I DO NOT GO TO SEE VICTOR. Adèle comes to see me.
Madame Ladame delivers the message with my morning coffee.
A hastily scribbled note from my beloved, asking me to meet
her in the Jardin du Luxembourg at noon.

Who sees love arriving? Who can gauge the movements
one person makes towards another? Movements so slight, so
tentative, that they almost seem to be invisible.

Who sees love arriving – but who doesn't see it leaving?

Adèle is waiting for me when I arrive at the gardens. She
is pacing between the statues, staring at the ground, in much
the same way Victor's mistress was studying the stage floor the
night I went to see her disastrous performance in *Marie Tudor*.

I am almost upon Adèle before she notices me. She stops.
I stop. It is so long since we've seen each other that all the old
endearments wither on my tongue.

"Charles," she says, "you've come."

"Of course."

She holds out her hand and I take it shyly.

"Walk with me," she says. "I am too restless to sit."

It is a cool afternoon. The sun disappears behind clouds,
peeks out again. Because it isn't a fine day, we might be the only
people in the orchard. Adèle and I walk along the gravel paths,
past the ornamental maze, towards the orchard.

"Victor has a mistress," says Adèle.

"I know."

"How do you know?"

106

"It is the talk of Paris." I decide not to mention going to see Juliette Drouet in Victor's play.

Adèle stops me with a hand on my arm. "Do you think we were ever the talk of Paris?" she asks.

"I'm not sure. Probably not. I don't think we're as…" I search for the right word. "We're not as blatant as Victor."

"Boastful, you mean."

"Confident," I say. "We're not as confident as Victor."

We reach the orchard. I look at the tags on the apple trees without comment. Our game belonged to those halcyon days before I told Victor of my affair with Adèle. There's no point in even mentioning the apple names now. We walk past the Great Unknown. Both of us look at it, and both of us look away.

"Is that it?" I ask Adèle. "Is that why you haven't come to see me, or sent word of how you are? Is that why you're so agitated now?"

Adèle stops on the path. "Victor's mistress is retaliation for my affair," she says. "But it's made him happy."

"Happier than we were?"

"Were?"

"You haven't come to see me, Adèle." I don't mean to, but I sound petulant as a child. "I have nothing but memories these days."

"Isn't that what we're left with in the end anyway?"

"No." I think of my morning routine in the Hotel de Rôuen, the comfort ritual bestows. "We could have a life together reinforced with small gestures, kindness and tenderness. We could have a life of shared experiences."

"Could we?" Adèle puts her hand on my arm. "I've given you nothing but scraps, Charles."

But they were beautiful scraps. They were scraps made from the finest lace. I think of her wedding veil, folded and tied with ribbon, kept in my desk drawer with her letters.

There was a time when I would have buried my hands in

Adèle's hair, when I would have begged her to come away with me, but something has happened to me in her absence. I have spent months in solitary confinement, writing my novel. My thoughts have become solitary thoughts, my movements solitary movements. I have been writing about my love for Adèle, and perhaps, in some strange way, the writing has replaced the actual love.

"You can't do this any more." I say it for her.

"No. I can't do it any more."

The sun goes behind a cloud (how appropriate) and the air blows cold across my skin. Adèle's hand on my arm feels heavy, and I want to throw it off, throw her off and storm down the path, disappear into the trees. But I understand everything. I am weary with the burden of understanding everything.

"It's not fair to you," says Adèle. "You could marry."

"Please," I say, to stop her from continuing along this line. I am an ugly man. I have a sex the size of a snail. Most people don't like me, certainly not after they get to know me. I am arrogant and reckless and foolish. Sometimes I change my mind about what I am saying in mid-sentence. I can write moderately well, but that isn't enough to save me. "I will never love anyone as I love you."

"Nor I." Adèle takes her hand from my arm and I already miss her touch so acutely that my eyes tear up. How will I bear it? I am a weak man and not possessed of great strength of character. I am not equipped to handle the abandonment of love. Because of my secret I will probably never find someone who accepts me as Adèle has accepted me.

Later, of course, I can see that Adèle had no choice. She will be punished for her affair with me all her remaining days, by Victor's infidelities and his flaunting of them. She cannot leave her children, or the financial security of her marriage. The selfish thing would have been to hang on to me. It was actually an act of generosity to release me.

But now all I feel is the dull smack of grief, knocking me to my knees in the gravel.

Adèle kneels beside me, wraps her arms around me.

"Don't cry, my love," she says. "I'm so sorry that I've hurt you. I will never forgive myself for that."

My sobs make talking difficult, even if there were something I could bear to say. I lean into her last embrace, and shut my eyes.

This is what I've learned about life – that things go on as they begin. Adèle and I never had enough time to be together, and in retrospect I can see that it was only going to get worse. The situation was stronger than we were. It was only ever going to end the way it did, with both of us on our knees.

We parted there, in the orchard. I stood up and went one way down the path. She stood up and went another way. The day, ironically, brightened.

But just as animals are restless when they're ill or anxious, I couldn't settle. I couldn't go back to the Hôtel de Rouen and resume my work. Writing requires a certain kind of peace, the reassurance that one can leave this world to enter the world of the book and return to find things more or less the same. I was in too much distress to be able to trust in that.

I walked through Paris. I walked to the little church where Adèle and I used to meet, although I was too heartbroken to enter. I walked to Notre-Dame and circled the outside walls, not daring to go in there either. To venture indoors would be to have my sadness constrict around me. At least when I was outside there was space for it to dissipate, to be carried off by the breeze from the river, or burned from me by the heat of the afternoon sun.

I walked to our old houses on Notre-Dame-des-Champs. I stopped only moments outside mine, but I stood for a long time in front of Adèle and Victor's.

There is the window of Dédé's room, where Adèle and I first made love.

There is the window to the parlour where I would sit with the Hugos at night, discussing literature for hours, reading Victor's poems before they were to be published.

There, through the gate, is the garden where I would visit Adèle and her children, where I would linger longer than was necessary, wanting never to leave her presence.

There, at the gate, is where she ran after me, the night after the day I fought my duel with Pierre Dubois. "I couldn't live without you," she said.

It is an otherwordly feeling to be held by arms that will no longer embrace you, to stand in front of a door that once admitted you, but is now barred to you. I felt as though I were already dead.

Places exist as monuments to the feelings that were revealed there. The entire Hugo house on Notre-Dame-des-Champs is a memorial to my love affair with Adèle Hugo.

Pretty white flowers twist through the garden gate. I pick one and thread it through the buttonhole in my waistcoat. Much later, when I have occasion to look it up, long after it has died, I find out that it is not a flower but only a common weed.

PARIS, 1840s

CHARLES

I HAD THEM PRINTED. What can I say? My poems were too good to keep to myself. I always considered them to be my greatest achievement.

Their subject was Adèle, and my love for her, and in the poems I named names and places. I made no move to hide anyone's identity. I had the book privately printed in 1843, five hundred copies.

I had meant to keep the copies locked up in a cupboard until Victor died. But Victor seemed as vigorously healthy as ever, and so I distributed a few copies of *Livre d'amour* to my friends. It was the one literary work in which I still felt great pride.

Adèle, of course, had seen some of the poems when we were together. She loved me so she had not minded them, although she often tired of listening to them. I think she was forced to listen to an abundance of poetry in her life with Victor, and she wanted me to offer respite from that, not additional torment.

I wanted to send Adèle a copy of the book when it was printed, but I feared that it might fall into the hands of her husband, and I could not risk that. Somehow it reached Victor anyway. Word came to me through a mutual friend that Monsieur Hugo was outraged, and that his oldest son, Charles, my namesake, although only seventeen, wished to challenge me to a duel.

Mercifully this did not happen. But suddenly all of Paris

loathed me. When I walked in the streets I had to keep my eyes on the gutter in case I met with an enemy. Even my housekeeper said she heard spiteful talk of me when she went to the market.

Ironically enough, I was no longer in hiding from the Garde nationale, and had moved back in with Mother, but I would have been better served if this were still the case.

Can a man not write the truth? Can a man not call his love by name? The gossip that my housekeeper rather delightedly reported back to me was all about my indiscretion and indecency in detailing my love affair with the wife of Victor Hugo. "How it must have shamed him," one man put it.

But *Livre d'amour* wasn't about Victor. I didn't mean to shame him. I wasn't thinking of him at all, truth be told. This was a book because of, and for, my beloved Adèle. I couldn't help the fact that she was married to Victor Hugo. I'm sure I would have loved her whatever circumstances she occupied.

But outsiders always see the situation, not the individuals. The literary elite of Paris no doubt thought that I was flaunting my affair with Adèle in Victor's face, that *Livre d'amour* was nothing more than a boastful taunt to the great man.

I suppose there was a little truth in that, but it was unfair that everyone judged my book on its scandalous content and no one saw its literary merit.

I still have great stacks of the book in a cupboard in my bedroom. Sometimes, late at night, when I am feeling particularly melancholy, I unlock the cupboard and look at the neat rows, the spines so uniform, the yellow paper of the cover so crisp and clean. I run my hands over the volumes, feeling the small indent where one copy ends and another begins. My masterpiece, like the great love that inspired it, is not allowed out in public. It remains hidden. I visit it at night, clandestinely, with the same excitement that I used to rendezvous with Adèle.

I HAVE BEEN INVITED INTO the prestigious Académie française.

Well, actually, it wasn't really that simple.

Let me explain.

The Académie française was established by Cardinal Richelieu in 1635 as an institutional body to oversee the use of the French language. There are forty seats. Members are elected for life, and when a seat falls vacant, one may apply to occupy it. There is an election and the successful candidate must deliver a speech eulogizing the dead man whose seat he will be taking. He is given a green jacket and ceremonial sword and is then welcomed with a reception speech given by another member of the Académie.

Aside from the prestige, there are practical reasons for being a member of the Académie. First, I will be able to charge more for any articles I write. Second, my book sales will increase. I could also be appointed to the Commission that works on the dictionary of the French language. It would be so satisfying not only to use the words of my language, but to control the words themselves.

So, when a seat becomes available, I put myself forward as a candidate.

Unfortunately, Victor is already a fellow of the Académie and he tries to block my membership by nominating Vigny, Dumas and Balzac. I campaign as best I can, soliciting the other members for their votes, but I fail.

It is deeply humiliating.

But shortly after, another seat becomes available when Casimir Delavigne dies, and I am encouraged to put my name forward again.

This time I am successful.

I am to occupy seat number twenty-eight, which is thankfully nowhere near Victor, who is in seat number fourteen on the other side of the room. But he is seconded to deliver my reception speech, and although he postpones doing it for the better part of a year, he can't put it off forever, and on February 27, 1845, we both arrive at the Académie with what, I'm sure, is a mutual feeling of dread.

I wear the green uniform (which I rather like) and even strap on the ceremonial sword, although it bangs against my leg in a most annoying manner when I walk.

The room is crowded, overcrowded in fact. I have difficulty in securing a seat for George.

"There are so many spectators," she says. "Because everyone in Paris knows that there is no love lost between you and Victor, and we can't wait to hear what he will say about you."

I sit down in my seat. Victor stands up in his. The crowd murmurs and hushes. My sword presses against my leg, cutting off the circulation below my knee.

Victor is older and fatter now, as am I. He has a beard and stands with his chest pushed out, clearing his throat before he begins to talk. It is not as I had feared, and I realize now that Victor cannot condemn me in this place. I have been elected a member, and it would be extremely bad form to insult me in front of the other members. He has his own image to think of. But he does not praise me highly either. While he says some nice things about my work, he lavishes his most passionate oration on the physicality of the books themselves.

"The bindings of Sainte-Beuve's books are exquisite," he says. "The best Moroccan leather, and gilt-edged as well. No expense has been spared in bringing his words to the public."

He sits down. There is tepid applause. Afterwards, he finds me in the lobby outside the meeting room.

"I hope you are happy," he says. "Taking yet another thing from me."

"Victor, you don't own the Académie. Only seat number fourteen."

In our green jackets, decorated with laurel leaves, we look like stout forest people about to scavenge for nuts.

"You ape me," he says. "You want to be me."

"No, I don't. Have you forgotten it was my praise of your poems that made your name?"

There is a flicker of something on Victor's face. Sympathy perhaps. No, pity. No, disgust.

"Can't you see, Charles," he says, "that I didn't need your approval? I would have become great without you. It was just a matter of time. You did not grant me any favours. I took what was rightfully mine."

It was more a matter of opinion than a matter of time, I think, but he has already turned away from me. I want to rush after him and run him through with my ceremonial sword, but I turn away as well.

Because there is some truth in what Victor has said. But I do not want to *be* him. He has that wrong. I want to be better at being him than he is. I want to love his wife with more respect and reverence and tenderness than he is capable of giving her. I want to offer myself to words, not try to bend them to my will. I want to be grateful for my place in the world, not feel that success is my birthright.

It turns out that the Académie is disappointing. What can I say? Everyone talks at once, like schoolchildren without a teacher. I never enjoy the meetings, even though I never stop enjoying the uniform. The meetings are not about what anyone says, but merely about who can speak the loudest.

~~~~~

Surprisingly, Mother is very impressed with my entrance into the Académie française. She faints when she is told the news, and then rushes out with an armful of flowers to lay at the feet of the Virgin in her local church.

So, when the small town where I grew up decides to honour me with a reception, she will not be stopped from coming.

I have become the most famous person to have lived in Boulogne-sur-Mer. It is mostly a town of fishermen, of commerce based on the sea. I don't imagine that anyone there actually reads my writing, but it is kind of them to want to honour me, and I am touched by their kindness.

The Mayor has decided to hold the reception in the bakery that occupies the ground floor of the building where Mother and I used to live. I still remember the warm smell of the pies rising up the staircase to our apartment.

"Do you remember, Sainte-Beuve, how you used to stick your fingers in the tarts so they were ruined and would be given to you later for free?" says Mother, much too loudly and in front of the small assembled crowd. Everyone laughs.

"Please," I say. But Mother, who has never received anything like applause before, finds the laughter of the crowd very stimulating.

"He was such a naughty little boy," she says. "Ruining the tarts. Keeping secrets. Telling lies. Never doing what he was told. Lazy as a hog. Always lying around reading those tiresome books."

More laughter. The Mayor steps forward and awkwardly drapes a red sash across my shoulders. "For your books," he says. There is a smattering of applause. Glasses of champagne are offered to everyone. The baker's wife passes around a tray of tarts. I dare not take one.

I leave Mother in the bakery, go down to the sea to walk

along the shingle. The wind blows hard from across the Channel, wraps the red sash around my neck like a scarf.

Across the Channel lies England, a place I went to for a month once. It excited me to go there. There was English blood in my family. My mother's mother, whom I never met, was an Englishwoman named Margaret Middleton.

But the actual experience of England was less ecstatic than the imagining of it. I stayed in a country house in Alvescot, near Oxford, having been invited there by two English brothers who were friends of mine at school. The family, unfortunately, was given to exercise, and I was forced to tramp about in the rain and even, on one terrible occasion, to attempt riding. The food was practically inedible. There was an alarming amount of shooting and fishing, and everyone I met seemed to be a parson, although none of them very devout. The one redeeming grace was my introduction to the Lake poets – Coleridge, Wordsworth, Collins – and I decided to translate a few of their poems into French when I returned home.

But my translations are no consolation now. It is ironic that, at a point in my life where I feel I have lost everything, I am suddenly being rewarded for my accomplishments.

The fishermen are returning from their day at sea. I stand in the shelter of a cove and watch the boats sailing towards the beach. As a boy I used to come down to this very spot and gaze at them. I liked the shouts of the men as they compared their catches. I liked the intricate lace of the nets, pegged out and drying in the sun.

None of these men will ever wear the green jacket, or be draped in the red sash, but nor will they ever care about these things, or see the merit in them. What is an honour if it means something to only a small group of people? I will never be someone whom these fishermen will want to know.

~~~~~

Mother is jubilant all the way home to Paris in the carriage. She bubbles over with talk. I look out the window, watching the countryside judder slowly past.

And then, suddenly, unexpectedly, there is the feeling of poetry in me, rising as fervently as desire. Even though everything is lost, perhaps something of what is lost is still recoverable. Perhaps, even if I never visit my birthplace again, I can find a way to describe the sound the fishing boats make when they beach on the shingle after a day at sea and, whenever after I read that passage, that image will return to me.

And that is better than any honour I could be given.

The boats heave themselves up out of the sea, like strange wooden fish, the hulls hitting the beach with a great booming sound. No, not fish, it is more that the hulls are waves, but heavier than water. The booming sound they make when they are thrown forward from the sea onto the beach is like the sound of a bell. It is deep and sonorous, and the whole fishing fleet plays a madrigal of bells as it comes to shore.

The red sash that the Mayor gave me is still wound around my neck. I unwind it, fold it carefully into a small rectangle and hand it over to Mother.

"I want you to have this."

"Oh, Sainte-Beuve." For a moment she is actually speechless, clasping the piece of red satin against her bosom. "What a day!" She carefully puts the folded sash on her lap and fumbles in her bag. "I have something for you too." She passes me a box.

"What is it?"

"Open it and see."

I lift the lid, and inside are four tarts from the bakery, nestled in straw to keep them safe from breaking.

I AM THE LIBRARIAN at the Mazarine Library in the French Institute on the quai de Conti through most of the 1840s, and I have been given rooms to live in at the Institute. By day I sit at a desk and enter into a ledger the names of those patrons who come to borrow books from the library. By night I sit up in my rooms, reading and writing. I have arrived at a life entirely circumscribed by literature.

I was offered the job through a rather strange set of circumstances.

It all started when Louise Colet, who is the mistress of both Victor Cousin, the politician and Gustave Flaubert, the novelist, was savaged by the critic, Alphonse Karr, in his monthly satirical journal.

Louise Colet did not take kindly to being ridiculed in the press and she called on Alphonse Karr at his home. When he turned from the door to usher her into his apartment, she took out the kitchen knife she had concealed beneath her skirts and stabbed him in the back.

He was not killed, but in an effort to have the whole unpleasant business quietened down, Victor Cousin, who was the Minister of Education at the time, asked me if I would speak to Alphonse and convince him to let the matter alone.

This was more easily done than I had imagined, as I think Alphonse was genuinely shocked and terrified by the stabbing, and by the fact that it had made him afraid. But I argued that to make more of the assault by laying charges would be to entertain those feelings longer than he wanted. So he decided to let the matter rest, contenting himself with displaying the knife in a glass case inside his home with the inscription: "Received from Louise Colet – in the back".

As a reward for my part in the case, Victor Cousin gave me the position of librarian in the Bibliothèque Mazarine. I receive housing and 4,000 francs a year, all for the trifling inconvenience of sitting at the library desk two days a week. Victor Cousin is very generous with his appointments. He has also given Alfred de Musset a position as librarian for the Ministry of the Interior – which has no library.

So here I sit, at my little desk under the vaulted library ceilings. Footsteps occasionally echo through the passageways, but mostly it is silent in the library. The new outbreak of cholera has kept a lot of the patrons away.

Sometimes I entertain the fantasy that Adèle will come to the library, completely by accident, but here my fantasy always has to end for I know that Adèle would have no interest in visiting the Institute de France. She has had enough of books. The literary life has not exactly served her well.

When I am bored with sitting at the desk I walk the library, trolling my fingers along the spines of the books, the way I would ripple my hand down the iron fences when I was a boy. The spines of the books are like the bars of a fence, like the bars of a cage.

I stand before my own books and think of all the hours and days and years that have gone into these small volumes. How inconsequential it all seems. To what purpose have I given my life away?

And if I am feeling in a particularly melancholy mood, I will go and stand in front of Victor's books, which occupy the better part of one whole shelf. They are like a small wall in front of me. A barricade, like the barricades the revolutionaries build in the streets these days, and crouching behind them to throw rocks at their enemies.

Victor, of course, has become the hero of the new revolution, the one that started four years after we met. He has so much public sympathy that he will probably run the country one day. Such is his need for admiration. I understand his desire to be famous, but not the fact that he *is* famous. Why? His books are no better than anyone else's. He is not set apart by his peers as the best writer of the day. This honour probably belongs to Flaubert, or God help me, that fat braggart, Balzac.

What is it that makes Victor's ascension so swift and sure? Is it luck? Is it timing? Surely, if one did not know of his reputation and read one of his novels alongside my own, the under-appreciated *Volupté*, there would not be much difference in the quality of the books. Why then do I languish in obscurity as a novelist while Victor continues to rise to glory? Why do I have to spend my days being a librarian?

Before going to bed I stand by my window in my night-shirt, looking down into the little courtyard below my rooms. Sometimes I can hear the rattle of the death carts carrying the new cholera victims from the neighbouring streets. I try to ignore that terrible sound, and look instead at the small fountain that protrudes from the courtyard wall. I like the murmur of the water, and the figures on the fountain – Eros playing with a butterfly. It is such a lighthearted scene that I am grateful it is there for me to gaze upon.

I always leave the window open when I sleep, just a fraction, so that I can feel the cool night air on my skin, and so that sometimes, if I wake in the dark, afraid and alone, I can let the whisper of the fountain rock me back to sleep like a lullaby.

I mention revolutionaries and death carts. The 1840s have brought more political change to France. The population of Paris has doubled since 1800, leading to overcrowding, unemployment and disease. In the end, cholera will kill over 19,000 people in two years.

One day I was walking near the Place Vendôme when I came upon a crush of men armed with paving stones and sticks. I ducked down a side street, but there were more of the revolutionaries there. Luckily I spotted my old acquaintance, Alphonse de Lamartine, coming out of the back door of the Hôtel de Ville. He was now one of the revolutionary leaders, having traded his pen for politics. And he was very popular among the people.

The mob saw Lamartine at the same time as I did. They pushed towards him. I pushed towards him.

"*Vive Lamartine!*" they shouted. And then one of them spied me and yelled out to the others. "A priest! A priest in disguise!"

I could feel their hands upon me, and I swear they would have torn me to pieces like a pack of wolves if I hadn't reached the safety of Lamartine, who ushered me into his carriage and drove me away from the mob. But next time there might be no one there to save me and I could be killed by the members of a cause to which I have actually given my support.

Best to stay indoors for a while.

Because, aside from the mobs, there is also the cholera. In time, Napoleon III will widen the streets and create huge new boulevards to replace the warren of medieval Parisian alleys of the 1840s. But for now, those narrow streets, airless and sunless and burdened with heavy traffic, cause so much disease. Gutters at their sides are intended to carry the garbage and raw sewage to underground viaducts, but this happens only when it rains. The rest of the time the garbage and excrement lie open to the air, and in the evenings the gutters are overrun with rats and mice, feasting greedily on the vile soup.

George has fled to her country house. During the 1832 epidemic she had lived across from the morgue on the Ile de la Cité, and had watched the endless procession of death carts, each one piled high with bodies.

"I couldn't stop watching," says George, when she comes to say goodbye on her way to her country estate. "I sat at my window all day. It was so compelling, and I felt obliged to witness this last journey of the poor souls who had died. I just can't stand to see any more death."

I worry for Adèle, but I hear no word of her fate.

I HAVE WRITTEN ANOTHER book of poems. It was completed quite soon after *Livre d'amour* was published privately and borrowed much from that book. In the introduction I have written that friendship is still the main subject of the verses, even if it is not, any longer, a single dominant friendship.

What a convenient word "friendship" is. It is a blanket to throw over one's more naked feelings.

I have called the little book *Pensées d'août*. The title is literal, as I did write much of the book at the end of a summer. August is the hinge between summer and autumn, a time of bitter-sweet change. The days are still warm, but there is the awareness that winter is coming, and one day, just in one day, everything changes and one wakes to find that the air has a chill in it, and that a coat is now required in the evenings. I think that this is the natural season for contemplation, and that poetry comes from this spiritual August – this place between loss and arrival. The emotion disappears and the word moves in to take its place. The last flowers of August thrive in the last of the summer heat, but they will not bloom again until spring. When one walks through the gardens and sees them, the joy at their existence is balanced, in equal measure, by the sorrow of their imminent departure.

Is this not the very condition of the human soul? Is this not what people hold within them at all times, this delicate balance of happiness and melancholy?

The difference between this book and *Livre d'amour* is that the former was written in the midst of love and hopefulness, while *Pensées d'août* is composed from the ashes of that love. Because of this, *Pensées d'août* is a very difficult book to write. Every time I sit down before the blank page, I must visit this loss, must experience it anew. It leaves me shaken, and sometimes, at the end of the day, the page on which the poem is written is blotted with my tears.

Sadness is selfish. It wants you all to itself. I shun human company, preferring the quiet consort of books. Every day when I write I feel that I am using up the words I have in me for that day, and therefore I have nothing left for conversation. My time is spent in this melancholy absorption, and it is not entirely unpleasant. The poems take my sorrow. They take all of it, and they transform it into something tangible.

I believe that poetry is about honesty. Say the thing that can't be said, and, if possible, say it right up front. During the writing of this book I take my signet ring to my jeweller and have him engrave the word "truth" on it. This is what I will wear on my body until my death, this single, implacable word. In English.

But truth is individual. My truth is not anyone else's. What I write is not necessarily to be believed, or to be appreciated by the people who read my poems.

So I write about myself, my feelings. My little book of verse does not sell nearly as well as the books by the great champions of the people – Hugo and Balzac – because, if you do not care to read about my emotions, then you will not care about my poems.

I am not clever like Victor, who pretends he is not writing about himself but is speaking on behalf of "the people". Really, his regard for himself is so large that it can be satisfied only by this idea that he is the voice for all humanity.

My book appears, enjoys a few reviews, and then disappears from the public's interest. One day, in a small second-hand bookshop not far from my old neighbourhood of Notre-Dame-des-Champs, I find a copy of *Pensées d'août*. I feel terrible that my book has been bought and dispensed with so soon after publication, so I purchase the copy. When I get home I riffle through the pages, looking for some clue as to why the owner of my little book would want to discard it so callously. There is no name inscribed on the flyleaf, no notes in the margins. The book is pristine and unmarked. But several of the pages have been carefully cut from the middle of the volume. I take down my copy of *Pensées d'août* and discover that an entire poem has been excised from the book. Well, someone must have loved the poem a great deal to remove it.

But if he loved the poem so much, then why not keep the whole book?

The answer lies in the poem. It is the one poem in the volume that directly addresses Adèle. So it is not hard to imagine that it was perhaps Victor, or one of Victor's friends, who has removed the poem. Not because it was beloved, but because whoever cut it out didn't want anyone else to read it. A small thrill whistles through my body. Have other copies of the book been purchased for the sole purpose of destroying this poem?

Perhaps I have a more interested readership than I had originally supposed. Perhaps Victor will buy up all the copies to keep the poem mute, and this sensation will increase my sales tenfold.

I LEAVE TO THE END OF MY recollections of this decade what happened at the start.

I have dealt with everything else in the 1840s before returning to this because I could not bear to write down the details of the event that has broken my Adèle's heart forever. You see, even though I believe in the truth, I am, in many ways, a coward, and I sometimes go out of my way to avoid meeting it.

In the winter of 1843 Adèle's oldest daughter, Léopoldine, was married to Charles Vacquerie. No one told me of this event, but I saw the notice of the wedding in the newspapers. Léopoldine was nineteen years old.

I had heard of the groom because his brother was Auguste Vacquerie, an avid supporter of Victor's. A disciple, really. He was a man with literary aspirations, and he had staged a new production of *Hernani*, probably with the sole purpose of impressing Victor. Why anyone would want to mount that dreadful play again is beyond me.

I suppose Léopoldine met Charles through the family's association with Auguste, although I heard a rumour that it was really Auguste who was in love with Léopoldine and that, at the wedding, he was in danger of proclaiming his love.

Life has a strange way of circling back on itself.

But Léopoldine was in love with Charles, and they married and moved to his family's village near Le Havre. Villequier, I think it was called. His mother had a house there.

In September, Charles and Léopoldine, along with one of

Charles's cousins, and an uncle, went for a sail on the Seine near the village. It was quiet and peaceful on the voyage out, but on the return journey a gust of wind capsized the boat and everyone aboard was drowned.

My Adèle must have cried as many tears as the amount of water in the river where her daughter died. It caused me tremendous pain to imagine her pain, and even though she had ended our affair, I felt compelled to go to her and help calm her suffering.

But this is not so easily done.

I know where the Hugos live in the Place des Vosges. Victor is so famous now that the apartment has infuriatingly been pointed out to me many times. It is on the second floor at the far end of the long, beautiful building.

I cannot simply knock on the door and present myself. I must go in disguise. I must go as Charlotte.

Mother's nervousness at walking in the Paris streets has resulted in her choosing only the most drab of clothes in which to venture out. I riffle through her wardrobe, trying to find something a little colourful, something that Charlotte would be happy to wear.

"Sainte-Beuve, what are you doing?"

I turn with my armload of dresses to find Mother standing in the doorway. I had thought she was out visiting Madame Fontaine.

I am caught. Mother does not know that I sometimes borrow her clothes, and I do not want her to find out. There would be no way to explain it that would make sense to her. She is a woman with little imagination. I am her son. She is not capable of thinking anything else. And even though she saw me naked as a child, saw the small winkle of my sex, she didn't think to consult a doctor. "All men are different," she had said to me, "below decks."

I must lie to Mother, and lie quickly. Not a single lie that she can dispute, but a barrage of lies, all coming so fast and furious that she will be bewildered by the effect and forget the issue.

"I thought I would have a dress made for you," I say, "and I was taking these to use as patterns for the dressmaker. There have been bed bugs in my room, so I wanted to have all our clothes laundered. You don't seem to wear these dresses much, so I thought I might give them to the unfortunate girl who begs in front of the church."

"Oh." Mother looks at the clothes, as though seeing them for the first time. "What are you doing in my room?"

"I just told you."

We stare at each other. Mother seems more stupid than usual these days. Perhaps she's losing what little mind she has left.

"Time for lunch, Sainte-Beuve," she says. "You should leave those here."

I bundle the dresses onto her divan and scuttle past her out the door.

I find a boy in the park outside the Hugos' apartment and pay him to take a note upstairs.

Will she come? I have signed the note as Charlotte so she will know who waits below her window, who paces up and down between the trees. My heart races and my mouth is dry. A small gust of wind pulls at the edge of my skirts.

Adèle is there in a moment. She runs from the door of the building, in her mourning dress, my note still clutched in her hand. Because I am not dressed in a way she will expect, she runs right past me and I have to call out to her.

"Adèle!"

"Charlotte?" She comes towards me, looking confused.

"Sister Charlotte," I say, for I am dressed as a nun. I bought the habit this morning. It was all I could think of to do. I couldn't risk getting caught by Mother again.

We walk to the far end of the Place des Vosges, out of sight of the apartment. We sit on a bench in the shade.

"I came as soon as I heard," I say.

Adèle turns to me. Her face is puffy from crying. She turns away again. "It's hard to talk to you when you're dressed like that."

"I'm sorry. It was the best I could do." I tug at the wimple which fits a bit too snugly around my face. "It's very hot in here," I say. "I had no idea that it was so stifling to be a nun."

Adèle manages a faint smile. "Not that it doesn't suit you a little," she says.

We sit in silence. I hold her hand. The wind moves in the trees above us.

"Little Dédé is only thirteen," she says, after a while. "We didn't tell her right away, and now she thinks that her sister is speaking to her from the grave. For days we knew Léopoldine was dead, but Dédé still thought her alive. Perhaps this is why she feels her sister talks to her; because at the moment of her death, Léopoldine *was* still alive to Dédé." Adèle shifts closer to me. "I don't know how to comfort her," she says.

"What about you?"

"What about me?"

"How can I comfort you?"

Adèle leans into me, her plump body slumped against mine, all weight and no vitality.

"There is no comfort for me," she says. "Just sit with me. For as long as we are able."

Once the proximity of her body would have sent me mad with delight. Now my body is simply there to hold up her sorrow, like a bolster on a bed.

What lives and what dies? The body dies, but the spirit of love persists. Love dies, but the body that tasted that love continues, absurdly, to exist. There is no knowing what will leave us and what will remain.

Perhaps this is the most frightening thing of all.

ADELE

THEY LEAVE THE BODY OUT FOR ME.

Madame Vacquerie meets me at the door.

"Prepare yourself," she says, her hand on my arm, leading me into the cavernous entrance hall. "She was in the water for a little while before they found her."

The house at Villequier overlooks the Seine, wide as a lake here where it feeds in from the ocean. The carriage drove along its banks on the way to this house. The water outside the carriage window a flat, blank sheet of grey and blue. No waves or wind today. A clear sky, and the river looking so picturesque, I had to keep reminding myself that my daughter had drowned there.

It has taken all night to get here, and I did not sleep, but sat up in the rocking, darkened carriage, preparing myself for this moment, a moment for which I will never be fully prepared.

Madame Vacquerie does not take her hand from my arm, and I am grateful for this. We do not know each other well, met briefly at the wedding a few months ago. We had spoken warmly to each other then, anticipating years of becoming acquainted, years of meeting up at the various occasions of our children's lives. In fact, with Léopoldine newly pregnant, we were expecting just such an event at the beginning of the new year.

"We have washed the bodies," says Madame Vacquerie. "And the graves have been dug in the cemetery. We could bury them tomorrow."

"Yes, tomorrow." I stumble on the lip of a doorway and Madame Vacquerie pulls me closer to her. She is practically holding me up at this point.

"A moment," I say, and I lean against the door frame. "I need just a moment."

"Of course."

We pause there. Outside I can hear the clatter of the carriage as it travels back down the driveway. My luggage must have been unloaded. It will be delivered to the bedroom where I will spend the next few days, a bedroom I have never seen. I wonder what it will be like? How odd to be thinking of that, to be thinking of anything except the fact that my oldest child is dead at the age of nineteen.

"Shall we go on?" asks Madame Vacquerie.

"Yes. I'm fine now."

We walk through a drawing room, lavish with red velvet drapes and two chandeliers, a life-size marble head of a man. There is a large book open on a table. We pass the table. It is a book of maps. An atlas. I can see the blue ink of the ocean.

"We have put her in the library," says Madame Vacquerie. "Charles is in the dining room."

It seems strange to have a body in the dining room, but then I realize that it is because of the table. Léopoldine and Charles will be laid out on tables. There would have been a ready table in the library, and another in the dining room.

"The coffins are made," says Madame Vacquerie, reading my mind. "But we thought you would prefer to see her in a more natural state."

"Is death natural?" I say.

The sun beaming in the windows of the drawing room fractures on the crystal of the chandeliers. I am momentarily dazzled by the shards of light dancing around the room.

Madame Vacquerie puts her arm around my waist.

"There is nothing worse than this day," she says. "I have

135

cried so many tears that I feel hollowed out."

"They were happy. Weren't they?"

"Yes, they were very happy."

We have reached the door to the library. The heavy oak door is open and I can see, in the dim interior – for there are no windows in this room – a white shape beached on a dark table.

Madame Vacquerie slides her arm from about my waist.

"I will leave you here," she says. "And I will wait in the drawing room for your return."

I don't want her to go. I don't want to have to enter that room and see my dead child. I don't feel able to make the journey by myself.

But Madame Vacquerie has already gone. She has sidled away, and I am left standing alone on the threshold.

Léopoldine is covered in a white shift. Her long black hair has been brushed out. Both my girls are dark like me. They resemble each other, and myself as a child. The boys take more after Victor.

I touch her hair. It's soft and dry. Funny, but I had expected it still to be wet, as though she would be preserved in the exact moment of her death, as though she had just been pulled from beneath the waves.

I touch her face. I touch her lips. Her eyes are closed. Her skin is cold and her skull feels hard and fast as rock.

"Sweetheart," I say. "My treasure. My little one."

My tears fall on her from above, like rain.

She seems like a statue of herself, but not herself at all. The girl who was Léopoldine seems utterly and entirely gone. I touch the stiff curl of her fingers. I touch the curve of her hip, the flat of her stomach through the shift. Her baby, no bigger than a stone, is dead as well.

I bend over my daughter as though I were tucking her in at night.

I touch her shoulders, her long, graceful neck.

"My little swan," I say.

I put a crucifix around her neck. I cut a lock of her hair with the small sewing scissors I have brought with me specifically for this purpose.

The room is dark. There are several candles flickering on the mantle, but their light is spilled close to them. Where Léopoldine lies is in shadow. In the soft darkness, with the candles nearby, and her white shift, my daughter looks like a moth. Her body looks like the body of a moth, wingless and still.

It would have been dark under water. As dark as this room. There would have been no sounds. She could not have cried out.

Madame Vacquerie is suddenly beside me.

"Come and have some supper," she says. "You must be hungry after your journey."

"I'm not hungry. And I don't want to leave my child. I just got here."

"You've been in here for three hours." Madame Vacquerie helps me to my feet. I've been crouching on the floor beside the library table. I can barely stand.

"Have I really?" It seems only a moment ago that I first saw Léopoldine, that I touched her face. But my body is sore from being curled up. My face is wet from crying.

I allow myself to be led from the room.

"How are you able to be so strong?" I ask Madame Vacquerie as she guides me back through the drawing room.

"I have had three days to grow accustomed to my grief," she says. "And I'm not strong at all. But I know how you are feeling right now. I know exactly."

"Thank you." It seems an entirely inadequate thing to be saying, but I say it again anyway. "Thank you."

We eat downstairs in the kitchen. We are served by the cook and sit at the servants' table in the middle of the kitchen, beside each other as though we were children.

I am unbelievably hungry. I eat the food the moment it hits my plate, although after I've eaten it, I can't even remember what it was I was served.

"Where is everyone?" It suddenly strikes me that we are alone, that Madame Vacquerie's husband and her other children are nowhere to be seen.

"I sent them all away," she says. "Just for tonight. They will be back tomorrow for the burial, and we will have a reception afterwards. But for tonight I thought it would be easier for you if you could be alone with me, and if we could be alone with our children."

"I would like to see Charles," I say.

"Yes."

The cook comes over with a slab of cake and cream. She places it carefully in front of me. "I'm sorry, Madame Hugo," she says. "I'm truly sorry."

Her kindness sets me crying again. I drench the cake with my tears, then I gulp it down.

Charles is dressed only in a long white shirt. His skin is as pale as Léopoldine's. His fair curly hair is as soft as a baby's.

"Are they pale from being under water?" I ask Madame Vacquerie. We are standing on opposite sides of the dining-room table where her son lies.

"I think so. And the water has made their flesh a little swollen." She gestures towards Charles's feet and I see that they are puffy. They look soft. I cannot see the bones in them.

"He is so beautiful," I say.

"My most beautiful child." Madame Vacquerie's voice catches.

"I had a child before Léopoldine," I say. "A boy. He died in infancy. We had called him Léopold, after Victor's father. It seemed natural to call the next child after that first one, but I wonder if it was right to name my daughter after a child who died."

Madame Vacquerie is stroking her son's hair. "We couldn't have done anything to prevent this," she says. "Even on the day it happened, I waved them off. They were only going for a sail. The weather was fair. The wind was low. Charles was a good sailor, and they were with his cousin, Arthus, and his Uncle Pierre who was a retired sea-captain and excellent on the water."

"They died as well?"

"Yes, they all died."

"What happened?"

"My husband thinks the boat was top-heavy with sails. It was a racing boat, had just won first prize in the Honfleur regatta. It was a fast boat. But the conditions were ideal. I don't know. The river is very wide there and those on shore couldn't get to them fast enough after the boat capsized. Your daughter's heavy skirts pulled her down into the water and caused her to drown."

I am quiet for a moment as I imagine Léopoldine struggling in a tangle of wet petticoats. Dresses do up so snugly at the back. It would have been impossible to wriggle out of one under water.

It is too painful to think of the moment of my daughter's death. Every time my mind goes there, I move it forwards or backwards and away from the event itself.

"Léopoldine would have felt very confident, going out on the water with such good sailors."

"Yes. She was looking forward to the afternoon."

Madame Vacquerie puts her hand on her son's forehead.

"Charles didn't die," she says.

"What?"

"He didn't drown. He surfaced. The rescue boat was close enough to see this. He was always a good swimmer. We live so close to the water that we made sure all our children could swim. People saw him surface, look around for his wife and call her name, and when he realized she was probably dead, he dived down to find her. He was found with his arms around her. They pulled them both from the water in a fisherman's net. He chose to drown with her rather than to live without her."

Charles's face is empty of feeling. He looks more serene, more calm than Léopoldine, but perhaps I do not know him so well. I do not know what his face is supposed to look like.

"Foolish, foolish boy," says Madame Vacquerie. "How was he to know that we grow out of that romance. An older man would never have chosen to drown."

My Charles would die for me, I think, and I realize that this is the first time I've thought about Charles since I got here, and that it feels wrong to think about him now.

"I'm so sorry," I say, because it is one thing to know that your child died in an accident and quite another to know that he chose to kill himself in the name of love. I would not have wanted that for Léopoldine. Her death, terrible as it is, will be easier to bear over time. Madame Vacquerie will forever question her son's decision.

"I wish your son had not made that choice," I say. "I wish he had loved my daughter less."

"You don't mean that," says Madame Vacquerie. "But thank you. It is kind of you to say it."

I don't mean it. I'm glad my child knew love if she was to leave this earth so soon. I'm glad she was married to a man who loved her, and who proved it in such a dramatic fashion. It can never be doubted. From this moment forward, it can never be doubted that Léopoldine was beloved.

"When should we have the service tomorrow?" asks Madame Vacquerie. "What time are you expecting your husband to arrive?"

At last the question I have been dreading.

"He's on a walking holiday in Spain," I say. "He won't be able to get here in time. We will go on without him."

I do not know where Victor is. He said that he was tired, that he had been working too hard and needed a change. So he left for a walking holiday in Spain. Usually, when he goes off by himself, I am relieved at his absence and have no reason to contact him while he is away. But when I tried to find him this time, at the hotel where he was meant to be staying, they said that he'd never checked in, that they had no reservation for him. It seems he is not walking in Spain. God knows where he is, but the lie means he is probably with his mistress, Juliette Drouet. He is with his mistress somewhere and he has no idea that his eldest daughter has died so tragically.

Léopoldine was always her father's favourite. He was more affectionate with her than with the other children. He thought her the most brilliant child of the four.

"It can't be helped," I say. "He will just have to miss the burial."

There's no response from Madame Vacquerie, and when I look over at her, I see that she is weeping. She is holding on to her son's hand and her head is bowed over his body. I back slowly out of the room without her noticing.

Léopoldine is as I left her, lying on the library table, still dead. It seems absurd that she should still be dead. I don't want her to be dead any more. I want her to get up, to move about, to become herself again. I want her to climb up out of the water and burst into the sunlight, opening her mouth to breathe in the sweet afternoon air. I want her husband to find her there, and to keep her afloat until the fishing boat arrives to rescue them both. I want them to have their child. I want it to be a girl. I want them to name her after Charles's mother. I want their married happiness to continue. I want there to be other children. I want to die with my eldest daughter as a woman in middle years, sitting at my bedside, holding my hand.

The candles gutter on the mantle, sputtering and flailing. The room grows darker and darker still.

It is awkward, but I manage to climb onto the library table. I lie down beside my daughter and pull her into my arms. She is stiff and cold. It is as if I am embracing the sea itself.

Did she cry out? Was she afraid? Did she know what was happening?

This was my girl, my first living child, who was talented and beautiful, who could paint and draw and write poetry to rival her father's, who had all the social graces, who was mischievous and kind and full of light, who had married for love. This was my child, this corpse, this heavy fish, this mermaid.

The day of the funeral dawns bright and clear. My bedroom is at the back of the house. Mercifully, Madame Vacquerie saw fit not to put me in a room that overlooks the river. My room looks down onto the gardens and the tops of the fruit trees in the small orchard at the back.

I had laid out my mourning dress the night before. A maid comes with a basin and some water. I wash. I dress. I see to my hair. I go downstairs.

Madame Vacquerie's family have returned. I don't know where she sent them, but it couldn't have been far. When I go downstairs, they are all in the foyer. The men bow to me. Monsieur Vacquerie says some words that I forget the moment he utters them. Charles's brother Augustus, one of Victor's most ardent disciples, asks repeatedly after my husband.

"He's not coming," I say, with more anger than I mean. Augustus nods and backs away from me.

I have slept later than I wanted. It is mid-morning. The bodies of Charles and Léopoldine were taken away late last night, to be placed in their coffins, to be readied for their burial today at noon.

Monsieur Vacquerie ushers me into the dining room for breakfast. The table that just yesterday held the body of his son, now holds cups and saucers, plates of rolls and steaming jugs of coffee.

Madame Vacquerie is seated at one end of the table. She nods to me as I enter the room.

"Madame Hugo."

"Madame Vacquerie."

She is formal with me. She is closed to me now. I can see it in her face. Her family have returned and her grief now belongs to them. Her husband passes behind her, places a hand on her shoulder. She puts a hand up to cover his, and the gesture makes me so lonely.

I eat more than I want to at breakfast, but again I am ravenous and can't help myself. Death has made me a glutton. Madame Vacquerie, on the other hand, barely touches her food.

Augustus tries to engage me in conversation about Victor, but I ignore him. When I have the opportunity, I take my leave and slink from the room, go back into the library and stand by the table where Léopoldine used to lie, sobbing until a maid comes to find me to tell me that my carriage is ready.

The words are said. The coffins are wheeled out to the open graves. The wind suddenly whips up when we are standing there, and the priest's vestments fill with air and make him look like a chess piece.

The words are said. The bodies are lowered. The words are

said. The dirt hits the wooden coffin lids, like rain lashing at the window on a winter's night. The words are said. The wreaths are placed. The hands are clasped. The wind subsides.

I stand at my daughter's grave to the end, after everyone else has left to go back to the house.

It seems impossible that Léopoldine is in this box, in this hole in the ground, and that I will have to leave her here, cold and alone, for all eternity. I can't believe it. I do believe it. I can't believe it. And it is hard not to think that this is punishment, that I am being punished by God for my sin of adultery, that Léopoldine was sacrificed because I am a sinner. It is hard not to believe this is my fault.

When I return to the house the reception is under way. I know almost no one, sit by myself in a corner of the drawing room, drinking tea and trying not to eat too much cake.

Madame Vacquerie is seated beside her husband. She sits up straight, talking to a young woman. I can see from her posture that she is holding herself upright, that if she didn't make this effort, she would collapse. At the graveside of her son, she fell to her knees in the dirt and had to be hauled to her feet by Augustus.

A mother's grief is not pretty.

I look around the room, at all the strange faces, at the chandeliers hanging from the ceiling. I look at the statue, the bust I passed yesterday morning on my way to the library, and I realize with a start that it is a bust of Victor. And I remember how upset he was to lose Léopoldine to marriage. He had sent her this head of himself as a way to assert his continuing presence in her life. Although, this was not how he had described it to me. He had told me that she would be lonely for him. Interesting that Léopoldine put it in a neutral place, the drawing room, rather than placing it in her private chambers.

But Victor did love his daughter. We loved her together. She was ours, and that bond between us will never be broken. From now on, we will be her archive. All the years of her life will be stored in our memories. She will only exist there. Victor and I are the only ones who have known her intimately since the moment of her birth. We will be more united because of her death, not less.

At that instant, a maid comes towards me from across the room. She carries a silver tray, and on that tray I can see there is a letter.

It is from my husband. He was in the south of France and read of Léopoldine's death in a newspaper while he was sitting in a café. He was travelling under an assumed name and never received my urgent messages, but now he is on his way to Ville-quier and asks me to wait for him. He ends the letter by saying, "My God, what have I done to you?"

Another woman might be confused by that phrase. Another woman might not wait for him. But I will be here when he arrives. I will greet him warmly. I will accompany him to the cemetery and show him where our daughter now lies. I will put my hand on his arm to steady him, as Madame Vacquerie put her hand on my arm to steady me.

And I am not at all confused by the phrase at the end of his letter. No, there is no confusion.

I know exactly what he has done to me.

CHARLES

MOTHER DIES AT EIGHTY-SIX. Increasingly frail, and increasingly demented, she lives long enough to see her body outlast her mind.

In the end she was afraid of almost everything. But her loss of memory made us better companions. She no longer cared what I was up to. There was no need to comment on my dress, or my habits. We became strangers under the same roof, but we liked one another better because of that.

My last good memory of Mother took place a few months before she died. I had come upstairs after lunch to find her standing perfectly still in the hallway. She had lost weight recently and her clothes hung loosely from her frame.

"What's the matter?" I asked.

"The street is so busy today," she said. "I don't know if I can get across safely."

I offered my arm. "I'd be happy to escort you."

"Thank you, monsieur. That is very kind."

She linked her arm through mine and we walked slowly down the hallway towards her bedroom, her feet shuffling along the polished wood floor. At her doorway she removed her arm from mine. I bowed. She smiled up at me, her face suddenly joyful, an expression of hers I hadn't seen since I was a child.

"What good fortune I have," she said. "To find such an obliging young man to help me."

~~~~~

The last time I see Victor it is by accident. In 1849, we are at the funeral of the once-famous actress, Marie Dorval, who has died run down and penniless at the age of fifty-one. During the church service, Victor stands on one side of the aisle, and I stand on the opposite side.

When I see Victor enter the church, I hope, for a brief moment, that Adèle is with him. But Marie Dorval was a friend of Juliette Drouet and, sure enough, it is Victor's mistress who accompanies him to the funeral.

The day is wet and grey. The service is depressing. Mother is dead and my contemporaries have begun to die off while in their fifties. I feel my own mortality advancing rapidly towards me as I stand with head bowed in the cold church.

George Sand is a few rows ahead of me. She is weeping noisily. Marie Dorval was a great friend of hers, and for a short time, even her lover. Well, that was the rumour anyway. I never did ask George if it was true. If she had wanted me to know, she would have told me herself. But she is weeping with enough feeling for me to believe that it was indeed true.

The novelist Balzac was the one who circulated the rumour through Paris. Balzac and I are not enamoured with each other because I reviewed him badly once. He hated my novel, *Volupté*, and told mutual friends that he could do a better job of it. Apparently his novel, *Le Lys dans la vallée*, is a rewriting of my book. I will not engage in his pettiness. I will not read it, even though I burn with curiosity. The irony is that, although his theme is stolen, his book sells better than mine. *Volupté* has not had the reception I had hoped for. Even George dismissed it rather cavalierly, calling it simply "vague".

But all that is behind me now. There is no more poetry in me. No more novels. I have become relatively famous, though it is not through those pursuits. I write a lengthy weekly biographical sketch in the *Globe*. These sketches appear on Monday and are called, correspondingly, *Lundis*. It has always been my opinion that to understand an artist and his work, it is necessary to know his biography. Some people do not agree with me. Marcel Proust, for example, argues that art can transcend the man. I don't see how he can really believe that art is delivered miraculously through the human vessel and not rooted in its material.

Others' opinions are not my concerns. I have my work to do.

My *Lundis* are short, well-researched biographies of great artists and philosophers – some living, many already dead. Each one takes a week to construct and write. They are wildly popular. Every so often, when I have written enough of them to be collected into a volume, they are sold as a book. My *Lundis* easily outsell my poetry and my "vague" novel, *Volupté*.

I find George outside the Eglise Saint-Thomas d'Aquin. She walks with me under my umbrella towards the row of waiting cabs. We are to ride to the burial of Marie Dorval in the Montparnasse cemetery.

"I'm sorry," I say. "I know you were close to her."

George hooks her arm through mine. Her face is streaked with rain and tears.

"Marie was so lovely," she says. "It never occurred to me that she would die. Her beauty should have exempted her."

George's comment makes me smile. "If that were true," I say, "then I would be long dead. If one could be spared death for beauty, then surely one would also be condemned to death for ugliness."

George squeezes my arm. "Ride with me to the cemetery," she says. "It has been so long since we've been in each other's company, and I have missed you."

But when we reach the road there is room for only one person in the first cab in line. It is raining so hard now that I fear George will be soaked to the skin while we wait for another cab to round the corner.

"I'll meet you there," I say, helping her up into the carriage.

I don't remember much of Marie Dorval except her close association with George. I saw her in several plays, but I cannot remember now what those plays were about. I do recall that in one of them she made a spectacular swoon backwards down a staircase, and the audience gasped in fear for her safety.

Love, I think. That's what love is – a backwards swoon down a darkened staircase. Well, no more of that for me, and no more of anything for poor Marie Dorval.

I still have the green umbrella with the yellow handle. A few comment on it. Many stare at it when I raise it. But I don't care. Let them mock me. It still keeps the rain off my body.

The next cab clatters up and I jerk open the door and climb inside. Someone is already in the cab, sitting on the small bench by the opposite window. A man in black, a top hat on his lap. I close my door. The driver flicks his whip at the horse and we lurch away from the church. It takes me a moment to recognize the profile of the man beside me, perhaps the same moment that it takes him to recognize me, for we both stiffen in apprehension at the sudden realization.

It is Victor Hugo who shares my cab. I'm not sure why Juliette Drouet is not with Victor. He must have been uncharacteristically chivalrous and dispatched her to the cemetery in an earlier cab.

I do not see Adèle any more. I do not know how she is, what she feels, what she does with her days. I do not see Adèle, and I blame Victor now for everything. It has not helped that he has become even more famous, that his literary ascension has been swift and sure. He has ended up with everything – fame, a family, a mistress. I do not understand why he should hate me as passionately as I hate him. I have lost our particular battle. But Victor obviously blames me for something. Perhaps his life is not as perfect as I imagine. He stares out of his window in the cab. I stare out of mine. The rain smears the glass and the streets wash by, each one leaf-strewn and wet, dark as evening.

If I were a younger man I would perhaps have made a pretence of conversation. We could have had a literary banter, or talked about the overwhelming sadness of Marie Dorval's death. If I were a braver man I might have brought up Adèle and asked after her welfare, told Victor something (what?) to let him know that my love for her remains virtually unchanged.

But as one grows older, one's character is reinforced by one's weaknesses, not by one's strengths, and if Victor plans to remain silent during our carriage ride, I am too much of a coward to break that silence.

The cab rocks along the narrow street, and it strikes me that I am still in awe of Victor Hugo, perhaps more than ever now because of his greatly increased fame. What I want to ask him, more than anything else, is whether he has read my novel, and what he thinks of it.

Pitifully, what I want to ask him is if he liked it.

Oh, how I hate this need in myself. Almost as much as I hate the man who could satisfy it.

The carriage rolls to a stop and Victor gets out without even a glance at me.

I LOSE ONE ADÈLE, and I gain another.

After my mother's death in 1850 I inherit the house on rue du Montparnasse. I hire a secretary to help with the research for my *Lundis*, and I hire a cook to keep house for me. The position of secretary has been rotated through a series of polite young men with literary aspirations. The position of cook belongs firmly to a new Adèle.

My work life is ordered; my home life is chaos. And yet they both take place under the same roof.

Once a week I dine out with my editor to discuss the subject of that week's *Lundi*. The next day my secretary comes to my house in the morning to talk over my new idea. We work in my bedroom. I sit at my desk, which in reality is two tables placed side by side. My secretary sits in a chair by the fireplace. Sometimes he is required to take dictation but usually, in the early stages of an idea, he is sent out to borrow books from the library and verify references, or he is simply there to listen to my thoughts. My ideas formulate more quickly if I am able to speak them out loud. When the article is written, I have my secretary read it out to me so I can adjust the phrasing as necessary. I find that my ear is a better judge of my words than my eye.

While we work, my cats prowl about the room. Only my favourite, Mignonne, is allowed to walk across my desk and disturb my papers. Sometimes she sits there, watching me write, her tail swishing from side to side rather angrily.

Charles Sainte-Beuve

My secretary leaves in the evenings, before my supper, and often I will walk out with him. We stroll through the Jardin du Luxembourg if the weather is good, tossing around ideas, detailing the tasks for the following day.

On the days when my routine unrolls without disturbance, I rise at five in the morning, shave without a mirror (so I do not have to look at myself) and don a dressing gown. I have become bald in my later years and so I wear a black skull-cap whenever I leave the house, and a black bandana inside the house. I wrap it around my head like a turban and I must say that, in that and my silk dressing gown, I look exactly like my mother. The resemblance is so striking that others have remarked on it as well.

I work from six to eight, and then I dress. If Adèle is awake, she will bring me a cup of chocolate and some bread. My secretary comes just after nine. At noon I have some tea and brioche, most of which I feed to the cats. In the evenings, after my secretary has gone home, I have a supper of bread and cheese, soup, meat and vegetables. I mix my wine with water. Once in a while I have a slice of almond cake that I buy from a baker on the rue de Fleurus.

Like my father, I write in the margins of my books. But where he used that space to carry on a conversation with the authors, I make notes that offer a shorthand interpretation of the text so that when I am looking for references, I can see, at a glance, whether there is something I will be able to use on that page.

As I have said, my work habits are orderly and comfortable. But that is not all that goes on in my house.

My cook, Adèle, is a drunk. It took me a while to discover this, and when I did, instead of being outraged at her behaviour and casting her out, I felt sorry for her and despaired that she would ever be able to find another situation, so I have kept her on. Sometimes she is so drunk that she forgets to make my supper, and when I go down to the kitchen to enquire politely as to its progress, I find her passed out at the table, snoring noisily, her head laid down on the bare wood.

She steals my wine. Once I caught her handing bottles of it through the kitchen window to one of her lovers, an omnibus conductor.

I must admit that I admire her unrepentance. On her good days she fills my house with flowers from the market. She is nice to the cats. Sometimes she sings to them while she cooks. Whenever she returns from the market they run downstairs to see what little titbit she has brought for them.

If it were only Adèle in my house, I could probably weather her thieving and her drunkenness. But often there are prostitutes living with me as well. Sometimes there is just one, and sometimes as many as three. Don't misunderstand, they are in my house not because I want them to service me, but rather because they have fallen on hard times and I feel pity for them. I want to offer them a harbour so that they can shelter for a while before venturing back into their calamitous lives. It is Adèle who tells me of these unfortunates, brings them to my house on Montparnasse.

Adèle is one thing. The prostitutes are another. They usually drink. They often fight with one another. Instead of appreciating my kindness, they treat me as though I am an idiot for taking them in, and rebuke me at every turn. One of them, a woman who was nicknamed "The Penguin" and had only one hand, was so rude to my guests that people stopped coming to my house. Even my secretary became nervous about entering. For the month she was there, I kept "The Penguin" confined to the downstairs. Even so, she would shout up through the floorboards, startling my visitors with her crudeness and insults. In the end I couldn't stand her behaviour and I sent her back to the streets, for which she seemed almost grateful.

I suppose I could take advantage of the prostitutes while they are in my house, but I'm always a little afraid of them and I fear they would laugh at my body when it was revealed to them. I've always been a little afraid of prostitutes. I have sometimes hired one to undress for me, but I have never dared do more than fondle her. So I try to treat the women in my house as ladies, although they are always very suspicious of this, and respond to my ministrations with open hostility. I have had saucepans hurled at me, and vile abuse. My mother's antiques have been broken. Anything valuable and small enough to carry has been stolen. Still, I persist. On Friday nights I take them all to the theatre, in the vain hope that it will instil some artistic sensibility in them.

At the moment we are mercifully between prostitutes. It is late. My secretary has left for the day and I wait, hopefully, for my supper to be delivered on a tray.

I wait, and wait, and then I trudge down to the kitchen to see what drunken disaster has befallen Adèle.

She is leaning up against the pantry door. Her skirts are twisted and her cap is crooked on her head. There is nothing cooking on the stove, no smell of supper rising from any of the pots.

"Food?" I say, hopefully.

Adèle fixes me with her gaze, then forgets to say anything.

The house feels airy and spacious without the prostitutes. Adèle's neglect is so familiar as to be almost reassuring.

"Don't worry," I say. "I will make myself some bread and cheese. I'm not that hungry tonight anyway." I cut some bread, put several cheeses on a plate.

"Wine?" I ask.

Adèle produces an open bottle from behind her back.

"Sorry," she says. This scenario has happened so often that apologies are entirely unnecessary, and I feel badly for her when she decides she has to offer one up.

I pour a glass of wine. I take down another glass and pour Adèle one.

"Come and sit with me," I say, "while I have my supper."

The kitchen is on the ground floor of the house. It's always dark in here, even with the evening light fumbling through the street-level windows. I light a couple of candles, place them in the centre of the table. Then I get a plate for Adèle.

"Thank you." She helps herself liberally to bread and cheese. We drink our wine.

"I saw another unfortunate," she says, "down by the river. Off her head with drink. Raving mad." It pleases Adèle to find women who are worse off than she is. She delights in it.

"Really?" My heart sinks.

"She has an infection." Adèle thinks for a moment. "No, affliction. She has an affliction."

"What sort of affliction?"

"The mental sort."

I chew my bread. "I can't be having an imbecile here," I say. "It would be too much work." I look at her. "For you," I say. "Remember the woman who imagined she saw rats everywhere? You never had a moment's peace."

"This girl is mental only because of the drink." Adèle holds out her glass and I dutifully fill it up. "And she's very young, barely older than a child. It would only be for a week or so."

This is what Adèle says about every prostitute who ends up staying here. More than likely this new girl will remain well over a month.

I sigh. "All right. Tell her to come round and see me."

"She'll be here tomorrow morning, monsieur," says Adèle, brightly.

"What's her name?"

"Claudine."

It's a pretty name. A name full of music and promise. But I have enough experience in these matters to know that Claudine will undoubtedly be thin and sickly, over-rouged, her teeth rotting in her head.

My friends don't understand why I take these women in, why I keep Adèle in my employ. I can't explain it to them properly.

Years ago I dreamed of living with Adèle Hugo. I dreamed that she would leave her husband and come away with me, that we would spend the rest of our days together. I remember the prayer I would offer up in the small church where we used to meet. *Please, God, let me live with Adèle.*

I didn't realize I had to be so specific. I didn't realize my prayer should have been *Please, God, let me live with Adèle Hugo.*

Adèle has come to me. My prayer has been answered. How could I possibly throw her out? And the prostitutes need help. They need a place to stay. Adèle feels powerful at being able to help them. I feel powerful at being able to help her.

I was afraid that I would die alone and lonely, and now I can be assured that will not happen. My house is full of energy and chaos. We are in full sail on this stormy sea.

"Shall we have some almond cake tonight?" I ask Adèle, refilling her glass.

"It's in the pantry," she says, and we stare each other down to see who will get up from the table to fetch it.

The happiness that comes to you is never the happiness you imagine. I never would have dreamed that I would know a one-handed prostitute called "The Penguin", or that the scent from the flowers Adèle has placed throughout the house would drift up the staircase with enough force to stop my hand above the page while I work.

"There you go," I say, setting the plate of cake down before Adèle.

She switches the plates around. "No, Monsieur," she says shyly. "That's not right. You should have the bigger piece."

Victor is in exile. He is living with Adèle and his children on the Channel Islands. Apparently his mistress, Juliette Drouet, is also there. He has secured a house for her near his family home.

Needless to say, Victor was a noisy supporter of the Republic. Since his election to the Académie française in 1840 he had become increasingly involved in politics. He campaigned for the Republicans. He spoke out against the death penalty. When Napoleon's nephew, Napoleon III, seized control of the government and instantly destroyed all the reforms Victor had worked so hard to establish, he was very upset.

Victor does not like to be opposed. I know this better than anybody. And the more famous he has become, the less he likes dissension, the less it agrees with him.

After Victor declared Napoleon III to be a traitor to France, the Hugos had to leave for Brussels. They then went to the Channel Islands, where they remain. Occasionally, Victor dispatches a political pamphlet on the ruination of France. Even though the pamphlets are banned here, they manage to be smuggled in. The political pamphlets, like all of Victor's work, are very popular. The last one was called *Napoleon le Petit*.

Of course, it was a shrewd move on Victor's part to go into exile, because now that he is absent from Paris, he just becomes more beloved, more valuable, in the minds of the people. It is as though he cannot take a wrong step. Everything he does advances his career.

Victor's exile, sadly, means Adèle's exile. It is fitting, I suppose, as the end of our love affair has felt like an exile anyway. Any small hope I might have had about Adèle's return to me has been dashed to pieces on the rocky shores of Guernsey.

I stay in. I go out. My habits, now the habits of years, are reassuring because they belong to me, but they offer less and less comfort. I have a restlessness that I can't find a way to settle. Even my cook comments on it.

"You've got mice in your underclothes," she says, one day when she comes to deliver my morning chocolate. "Look at you, all scratchy and full of the nerves."

I have been pacing back and forth in front of the window.

Adèle places the cup of chocolate on my desk without spilling any. She seems remarkably sober this morning.

"I can't bear to think of the Hugos on the Channel Islands," I burst out.

I picture my Adèle walking the windswept coastal paths, being blown off into the foaming sea. I see her floating on the surf, her hair tangled with seaweed, fish nibbling at her fingers and toes.

"What are the Channel Islands?" asks Adèle. Like most Parisians, she has little interest in the rest of the world.

We pore over the atlas. When my secretary arrives, I send him to the library for additional information. After her initial interest in seeing where the Channel Islands are located on a map, Adèle tires of the research and returns to her kitchen. But I won't let her be. I hurry down at noon, with my stack of books, thunking them on the kitchen table and making her jump at the stove. I'm out of breath from the stairs and it's the first time that I realize I get winded from going downstairs as well as up.

"I could definitely be dead within the week," I say. But Adèle doesn't hear me, or chooses not to.

"They're full of rocks," I say.

"What are?"

"The Channel Islands."

Adèle turns and regards me critically. She holds a wooden spoon in each hand. I don't dare ask her why.

"They're islands," she says. "They have coasts. Coasts are full of rocks." She speaks slowly, as though she's talking to her imbecile cousin.

The Channel Islands are a mix of French and English. I feel a brief twinge of envy. Victor is already famous in France. Now he will become famous to the English as well.

"There is no stopping him," I say.

Adèle puts down her spoons. "It is because you do not know," she says.

"Know what?"

"How it is for Madame Hugo. You do not know anything, so you imagine everything."

She is right. In some ways it would be easier if Adèle were dead. It would be finite. I would not be tormented by the endless possibilities of her existence.

I slam the atlas shut and drop myself down into a chair. If I am honest, it is not Adèle's safety that really concerns me. It is not imagining her being blown off a rocky headland into an unforgiving sea that causes me sleepless nights. It is imagining her happiness – her happiness without me.

GUERNSEY, 1850s

ADELE

I WALK OUT ONTO THE TERRACE. My children are still at breakfast there. They like to eat outdoors when the weather is fair. They like the bright morning light and the shuffle of sea against the rocks below.

"Maman!" calls Dédé, and when I go to her, she pulls me down beside her on the chaise. "What will we do today, Maman?"

If we were still in Paris, my children would be married by now. They would have lives of their own. But the exile has forced us to remain together as a family, and even though Charles, the eldest, is over thirty, and Adèle is a grown woman of twenty-seven, the isolation has turned them into children again and they look to me to lead them through each day.

I close my eyes against the sun, then open them and see the rag tied around the railing at the top of the house, the signal that Victor is up and working.

"Maman!" Dédé squeezes my hand.

"We could pick wildflowers on the cliff top," I say. "Charlot, you might photograph us up there, and you could bring your books, Toto. We could have a picnic."

Dédé drops my hand. "We did that yesterday," she says.

"But we had fun," I persist. "Did we not? And why not do something again if it was pleasurable the first time?"

There's a short silence.

"Yesterday wasn't the first time," says François-Victor.

"I might photograph in the garden today," says Charles. He

stretches his legs out, crossing his feet at the ankles. "Or I might have a nap."

He has grown plump, my eldest son. More often he declines a walk than accepts one. He is not like his father. Every afternoon, after he has finished his twenty pages, Victor will stride out across the cliffs to the sea to sit on the boulder he calls his *armchair* and gaze out over the waves, waiting to be inspired.

But the exile has been so good for Charles! He has time to indulge his desires, time to explore his interests, and the naps serve as *his* inspirational pause between artistic pursuits.

"Toto?" I say, turning to François-Victor. "Will you walk out with me today?"

"Perhaps." Toto does not like to disappoint, so he rarely commits to anything. I find this habit of his both touching and infuriating, so I refrain from commenting on it.

"Dédé?"

"No, Maman." Adèle has lowered her head in a sulk. I put my arm around her shoulders.

"Dédé, why don't you go and fetch your embroidery and I will help you with it. We could sit here in the sun. You could ask Sylvie to bring me coffee."

"Sylvie left," says Toto.

"For the day?"

"Forever."

"So soon?" The maid was barely here two weeks, and it was so nice to have a French girl for a change.

"Now it's Abigail," says Charles. "She's older."

"Should last longer then," says François-Victor, and they both laugh.

I ignore their comment.

"Dédé, go and fetch your embroidery." I give her a little push. "Never mind about the coffee."

"I'll get your coffee, Maman." Toto rises from his chair. I already know that he will not go for a walk on the cliff with me today, that this offer to bring me coffee is his apology for that. I am more than grateful to accept an act of kindness from my children. I squeeze his hand as he steps over his brother's outstretched legs.

"Thank you, my darling."

"Oh, *d'accord, d'accord.*" Adèle gets up, reluctantly, and follows François-Victor into the house.

It is suddenly so quiet on the terrace. I can hear the creak of a gull's wing as it flies overhead, and the rush and fall of the ocean below.

"Another day in paradise," says Charles, bitterly.

"Yes," I say to him. "Yes, I think it is."

We went to Jersey first, not Guernsey. On Jersey they spoke French. It was as simple as that. Victor felt that the Channel Islands were pieces of France that had broken off and been cast into the sea, only to be plucked out and claimed by the English.

In Jersey we rented a house that Victor christened "Marine Terrace". Like this house, it had a view of the sea, and like this house, it was haunted. The ghost of a young woman who had killed her child paced the halls, and sang in a sweet, melodious tone outside my bedroom door. She was known locally as the "White Lady" and Victor became so obsessed with her that he started to write love poetry to her.

We were under a spell on Jersey, I think, the long spell of Léopoldine's early death. When we were in Paris we could hold on to the memory of her. It was there in everything we saw, everything we did. Every room I entered in our apartment in Place Royale was a room I had been in with her. We did not have to work at remembering her. She remained with us. But here, out on the windswept Channel Islands, we could suddenly feel her gone, and so we tried hard to keep her close.

Victor had the dress she was drowned in displayed in the dining room of Marine Terrace, and we held nightly seances there so that we might speak with her.

Did I believe that she returned to us, that she tapped out words with the help of the table leg? No, I did not. The seances functioned as prayer for me. They created a space in which I could be with the memory of my beloved daughter. And they made me believe in the strength of our family. When we held hands around the table, I felt the love we had for one another, and for our departed Léopoldine. I felt that we were solidly together again in those moments.

But strength in excess can easily swing to weakness. And when Victor wanted to have three seances a day and invite any stranger he found in town to come and join us – when he thought he had summoned, not only Léopoldine, but Jesus Christ, Shakespeare, Napoleon and Hannibal to our house – I had to put a stop to the ritual.

Now I can see that it was a mistake to have indulged it for so long.

At one of the seances my youngest daughter, Adèle, met a penniless sailor named Albert Pinson. They quickly struck up a courtship and now, even though he has been posted back to England, and cannot possibly afford to marry her, she remains obsessed and will not stop trying to communicate with him.

Toto brings me coffee. Charles goes inside to his darkroom. I wait on the terrace for Dédé, drink my coffee, wait some more, and then I go into the house to search for her. She is by the window in the parlour, holding something up to the light, turning it this way and that. When I see the flash, I realize that she is holding the glass from her hand mirror, carefully removed from the backing.

"He won't see you in England," I say. There is nothing

out of the window but the endless blue of the sea. "He can't possibly see you from here."

Adèle won't look at me. She is intent on her signalling.

"Dédé."

"You don't know that he doesn't, Maman. You don't know what he feels."

We were three long years on Jersey, three years of sitting around the pedestal table and watching it tap out the alphabet against the wooden floor. I had not realized how impression-able my youngest daughter was, how those seances had trained her to believe in the intangible.

I slip my arm about her waist. "Come, child. Bring your embroidery out to the terrace. I will help you with your stitches."

Having first been expelled from France, Victor was then expelled from Jersey in the autumn of 1855 for organizing a protest against a visit the English queen paid to his enemy, Napoleon III. Because Victor was expelled, we were all expelled, and so we came here, to Guernsey.

I had thought that prolonged exile might dull Victor's loathing of the Emperor, but it has sharpened it instead. When he wrote his scathing pamphlet, *Napoleon le Petit*, he thought up many ingenious ways of smuggling it into France so that it might be read. It was stuffed into raw chickens, into carriage clocks, into bales of hay, into trunks with false bottoms, into shoes with false heels, into hollowed-out walking sticks and cigars. It was towed in sealed boxes below the waterline of fishing boats and thrown at night onto empty beaches. There was even an attempt to launch the pamphlet in balloons from the back of our house in Jersey, when the wind was blowing towards France.

The second exile has just confirmed everything Victor was

convinced of when we first left Paris. He remains absolute in the righteousness of his convictions. I do not believe that we will ever see France again.

Adèle's fingers are jumpy. They will not hold the stitches. I put my hand over hers to steady them.

"You are nervous today," I say. "You need some exercise. Come with me for a walk along the cliff."

Adèle puts the embroidery down beside her and leans into me. "Don't leave me, Maman," she whispers, and I put my arms around her and hold her close.

"I won't leave you, Dédé," I say. "You never have to worry about that."

I am blessed to have my children with me. I am blessed to have their company long past my entitlement to it.

We have bought this house here on Guernsey – Hauteville House, halfway up the steep hill from the town. It is the first house we have ever owned. Victor means to stay. He has been redecorating it since we moved in. He has built on the top of the house a glass box where he works. He has constructed a fireplace in the shape of a giant letter H, and made a large candelabra entirely of old cotton reels. He is so clever, my husband! There are tapestries on the walls. The rooms are painted rich, deep colours. One of the rooms is entirely devoted to the display of decorative plates. The ceiling itself is formed of plates. Victor insists on doing all the work himself. I think that if he weren't a famous author he would be a famous decorator. He has such a gift for it! But I will admit to not liking the Latin mottos he has burned into many of the ceiling beams. He does this with a red-hot poker, often late at night. I sometimes wake to the smell of burning wood and imagine

Hauteville House

that the house is on fire. But instead, in the morning, I will find a new, mysterious saying. Last week there was one added to the small downstairs lavatory. Victor had already decorated this lavatory with painted peacock feathers, and I do not understand why he felt the need to burn the words "ErrorTerror" into the room as well.

But the phrase I mind the most is the one carved into the wall just outside the dining room. *Ede I Ora*. It is what you see on your way into the dining room, and I think it would be much more appropriately placed within the room itself, so that you might see it on your way out. Eat. Go. Pray. The way it is positioned now makes it seem as though you will enter our dining room and be poisoned, and I feel embarrassed on those evenings when we have guests.

Tonight, mercifully, there are no dinner guests. It is just the family sitting round the massive oak table.

"Did the work go well today?" I ask Victor. I ask him this every evening. Every morning I ask him if he slept well. These two questions, and the corresponding answers, are sometimes all we have in the way of a day's conversation. We know each other so well, there is no need to talk at length! If Victor is feeling uncommunicative, he will answer simply *yes* or *no*. If he is feeling generous, he will elaborate.

"Very well," he says tonight. "In fact," he puts down his soup spoon, "I feel magnificently inspired from my walk today, and I think I would like to work on the biography this evening."

Victor's work is constant and self-generating. He could happily remain at his desk day and night, but the rest of us have had to take up various projects to keep us occupied during the exile. Charles claims to be learning to be a photographer. François-Victor busies himself translating the complete works of Shakespeare into French. Adèle is working at her embroidery, and playing the piano and composing music for it. I am writing a biography of Victor. Well, I am writing the biography, but Victor is helping.

"Of course," I say.

"Can you begin right after supper?"

"I can."

"But, Maman," says Adèle, "you promised that you would listen to my new piece of music tonight."

"Can I not do both?"

"No," says Victor, waving his soup spoon in the air. "I will not have my thoughts interrupted by that great wooden beast." He furrows his brow, puts the spoon down again beside his soup plate and fishes in his breast pocket for a small notebook. He swivels in his chair so that his back is to his family, and writes down what he has just said. He is so clever, my husband! He says so many witty remarks, and all of them will end up on the pages of his novels.

Adèle has her head bowed. I pat her arm, but she jerks it away from me.

"No matter, Dédé," says Charles from across the table. "You

can help me in my darkroom tonight. I think I have taken some good photographs of the garden this afternoon."

The biography is massive, and we're not even up to the production of *Hernani* yet.

Victor likes us to work on the dining-room table, after all the supper dishes have been cleared. He spreads out the pages of the biography and walks the perimeter of the table, surveying them. Sometimes he moves the pages into a different order. Sometimes he dictates a phrase or series of phrases, which I, seated at one end of the table, copy down. After we have finished working for the evening, Victor will gather up the pages and hide them behind the wood panelling in one of the secret cubbyholes that he had built when he renovated the house.

There is a restlessness to him tonight that makes me wonder if he really did go for his usual walk today. He moves quickly round the table, not settling on anything, his movements bending the light of the candle first one way, and then another.

"We will write a single day," he finally says, stopping just behind me. I can feel the heat from his body at my back.

"The day of the *Hernani* battle?" I say, eager to move the narrative along. At this rate we will have to do six volumes just to get to this present moment.

"No," he says, and he bends close so that his mouth is right next to my ear. "We will write about the first time we met Sainte-Beuve, that night he came to our apartment on rue de Vaugirard. You must remember that night, Adèle?"

"No," I say. "I don't. Not at all."

"Come now." His breath is in my hair. My hand tightens on the quill pen. "You must have a perfect recollection of the first time you caught a glimpse of our dear friend."

"No. I don't remember anything."

There is silence, and in that silence I can hear the growl of the ocean against the rocks and the tick of the clock in the hall. I can hear the quickened breathing of my husband, and the slick beating of my own heart in my chest.

"We were young and happy," I say. "That is what I remember. We were young and happy, and I wanted more than anything to be mother to your children."

This is true and we both know it.

Victor exhales and the candle flame leans away from us.

"The battle of *Hernani*?" I say. "We could work at documenting that day."

"Wasn't Sainte-Beuve there for that?" says Victor, but he moves away from me, continues down the table, and I know he has lost interest, so I can lie without being caught.

"No," I say, with conviction. "I don't believe he was."

That night I cannot sleep. I lie awake in my room, listening to Victor prowling around the darkened house. Usually he sleeps in his room upstairs, right next door to where he works so that he can rise in the night when inspiration strikes. For him to still be downstairs means that he has decided to redecorate something, or that he is going to burn another saying into the rafters of Hauteville House. I listen for the sounds of furniture moving. I sniff the air for the smell of scorched wood. But there is nothing. Perhaps it is the same restlessness that Victor displayed earlier this evening and he is trying to calm it by pacing. There must be something troubling occupying his thoughts.

I think back to our apartment on rue de Vaugirard. It was small and confining. The fire always smoked and the cooking smells were cloying. There was constant noise from the joinery downstairs. But that is not what I dwell on. Instead, I remember how Victor and I shared a bed, how we were rarely out of each other's arms, how his presence across the room would lift my blood to attention.

We might as well not be the same people at all.

It has been years, no, decades, since we shared a bed, or had rooms near to each other. I have slept next door to little Adèle ever since she was born, and Victor has made sure there were at least several rooms, if not floors, between us. If he entered my bedchamber now, I would be as alarmed as if he were a stranger.

That night on rue de Vaugirard, we were just sitting down to supper. I looked forward to our meals there. They were a welcome pause between our episodes of lovemaking, and they served to make me hungry to return to bed. I don't remember the meal. It would have been something simple. We did not have money in those days. Victor was a struggling poet. Soup or stew perhaps. Maybe some bread and watered-down wine. Often we didn't even have the money for that, and my sister, who lived nearby, would bring us round what was left of their dinner for us to eat. In spite of that, I don't remember ever feeling pity for our circumstances.

We were sitting down to dinner. The joinery had closed for the day and there was no more sawing and hammering, only the lingering smell of sawdust in the shared stairwell. We were sitting down to dinner and there was a knock at the downstairs door; a timid knock, such as a child might make.

I must have fallen asleep. I wake to the sound of knocking. It comes from the room next to mine. Dédé is trying to contact her dead sister in the spirit world. Every night she taps on the wall by her bed until she gets the response she has been waiting for. She has been doing this since Léopoldine died, even before the seances in Marine Terrace. She taps, a frantic patter, like the sound the heart makes after exercise, the beats so fast they are almost a flutter. She taps, and she waits, and in the silence before she knocks again, she is answered.

I try to stop Dédé from contacting Albert Pinson, but I am not able to tell her not to reach out to Léopoldine in the afterlife. This is the space she makes at the end of every day to be with her sister, and what right do I have to forbid this?

The house is quiet except for Adèle's tapping. Victor must have gone upstairs. There will be no strange Latin phrase awaiting me when I rise. His restlessness has found no earthly form tonight.

With morning there is purpose.

"I am going up to the cliff top today," I say to Dédé at breakfast. "I would like you to come with me, but I am going whether you come or not."

"I will go with you, Maman," says Dédé, her sweet nature returned. "And I will pick a very beautiful bouquet for you to put on your nightstand."

But when I go to collect Adèle after lunch, she is writing a long letter to Albert Pinson and will not be persuaded away from it.

"Could we not go later?" she asks, looking up at me from her work, her eyes wild and her fingers stained with ink. I can see a small stack of completed pages at her left elbow.

"But this is the best of the day. Right now. This moment. The heat will be gone later."

"Tomorrow then, Maman. Tomorrow most definitely." Adèle lowers her head, already lost to me.

The road that leads past our house to the cliff top is steep and I always have to walk slowly, stopping to catch my breath before I get very far along it. I always pause in the same place, outside a house with a lawn bursting with colourful flowers.

The flowerbeds twist across the grass, packed with the most exquisite blossoms. The blooms are more beautiful than anything we have growing in our sunken garden at the back of the house, and I envy their brightness.

Guernsey is barely ten miles long and only half as wide. Victor regularly walks the length of it. He is such a fit man, my husband! He has such vigour!

One side of the island, our side, is protected. The other side is wild and rough, open to the full wrath of the western sea. I don't often walk over to that side, preferring to stroll along the path that runs above our house and the sheltered port town that sits below that. But today the weather is clear and sunny, the wind is remarkably low, and I feel a borrowed restlessness from Victor. I leave the well-worn path at the top of the cliff and set out across the middle of the island along a sheep track.

On Jersey there was French society, but here on Guernsey the inhabitants are mostly English. We keep to ourselves, and the English in turn do not bother much with us either. Occasionally we have visitors from France, or some of Victor's Jersey friends will make the short voyage to our island. Victor enjoys guests and he has what he calls an "emergency" bedroom up in his glass tower, in case visitors arrive unexpectedly, or late at night. He has nicknamed this bedroom the "Raft of the Medusa" and it is quite frequently put to use.

I have no friends myself. The visitors who come to see Victor are never that concerned with me. I am lucky to have my family around me. Once my sister made the trip from Paris, but seeing her just made me lonely for home and, in the end, I wished she hadn't come.

The sheep track is deserted. I meet no one on my trek across the girth of Guernsey. I thought that I had come up to the high ground to pick wildflowers, but I seem to walk right by their weave and flash in the tall grass without hesitation. I seem to want to keep moving, to be able to get to the other side and back again before dinner. I will need to be in attendance when Victor climbs down from his tower. He likes to have his family gathered around him after a day spent alone.

The wind is higher when I get to the far side of the island. I stand on the edge of the cliff and the wind tears the breath out of my body. I sit down beside a rock and the force of the blast abates. The ground beneath me is soft with grass and thrift. I put a hand out and touch the rock, warm from the sun.

I don't know why I do it, but I lie down, there on the grass, with my body next to the boulder. The sky is endless above me, all blue like the sea, a few birds swimming through it, far out of reach. Perhaps it is because there is nothing above me that thoughts are released in me that have never struggled to the surface before. I do not think such thoughts in Hauteville House. I cannot. If I did they would be caught by Victor in his glass tower at the top of the house. He would net them as soon as they left my mind. They could not simply rise, undisturbed, into the open air.

I live in service to others, and because of this I do not often know what I think or feel. I say this, not as a regret, but as a comfort.

It is Charles I think of. Not that day, that first day, when he came to visit us in rue de Vaugirard. No, what I remember is a much more dangerous time than that.

I run from the rented château at Bièvres with the children's cries fading softly behind me. I run down the long cinder driveway, over the small bridge, to the edge of the wood where I know Charles waits for me. He hides there all day, preparing for the moment I can get away. And I don't care that Victor is probably watching me go from his room at the top of the house. I don't care that my children need me. I care only about reaching my lover.

And when I do find him, when he steps out from behind a tree or bush to meet me, we stagger together like drunks. Sometimes I don't stop running at all, just keep on going, smash right into him and knock him to the ground. Charles is so slight that it doesn't take much to wind him, and I like to hear the breath rushing out of him as I follow him to earth.

I cannot get enough of his embraces, of his kisses, of the way he pushes his face into mine as though he wants to become me.

Victor loves me. I know this to be true. But Victor loves me for himself, and Charles loves me for myself, and the difference between those two is so astonishing that I don't know how to reconcile them.

Charles holds my hand up to the sunlight. We are lying on our backs at the base of a huge tree. He holds my hand overhead, so that my fingers echo the pattern of the branches above us.

"You are as strong as that tree," he says. "I would like to be a little bird nesting in your branches."

"I wouldn't mind being a tree at all," I say. "It would be nice not to have to move."

"But you would move all the time," says Charles. He puts down my hand and rolls onto his side to look at me. "You would move with the wind."

"No, I would respond to the wind. I would answer it." I look up through the web of tree to the sky. "And only if I wanted to."

The demands of Victor and the children are incessant. They call and I must go to them, over and over during the course of a single day. I can never stand still, be still. I can never have a thought that is my own. Their needs have gradually replaced mine.

Already I have been gone too long from the house. I can feel the anxiety of this fact crawling on my skin.

I lower my hand to Charles's face, touch the skin of his forehead, pushing back to stroke his wispy hair.

"A bird would have a difficult time making a nest from your hair," I say.

"Yes," says Charles. "Soon I will be bald, and even uglier than I am now."

Charles will often describe himself as ugly and it pains me. I can only imagine that he heard this from his mother when he was a child and that pains me too, that she could treat him with such loathing. I think of my own children, how confident they are that they are perfect because I tell them so a dozen times a day.

I run my fingers over the sharp planes of his face, over the end of his hooked nose, around the soft contours of his lips.

"You are the most beautiful creature," I say.

I meet Charles in the forest. I meet Charlotte in the church. She is the only one there when I rush into the dark interior in the middle of an afternoon. She sits stiffly in the centre of a pew, eyes gazing straight ahead at the altar. Charles slouches and shuffles, but Charlotte has perfect posture. Her tiny shoulders are exquisite in that dress and I launch myself into the pew from the aisle, hurtling towards the unsuspecting Charlotte with the velocity of a cannonball. She turns towards me, smiles, offers a delicate, gloved hand – but I am well past such decorum. I have run down the staircase of the house, snagging the sash of my dress on the railing and just leaving it there, like the flag of a conquered country strewn on the bloody battlefield. I have heaved open the front door with such force that it banged back on its hinges, the sound reverberating through the entire building. If Victor was unaware I was escaping from the house, that crash would have alerted him most absolutely to the fact. I have tripped over the front step and fallen onto the grit of the driveway. There are still tiny indentations on the palms of my hands from where my body briefly married the shape of the gravel. I have flown down the road, my skirts fanning out beside me like wings, my feet barely touching the earth.

So when I hurl myself along the pew towards Charlotte, I am propelled by the full velocity of getting there. There is no stopping me.

"I won't wait," I say, one hand at her breast, the other already beginning to open her dress. "I will have you now."

The wind blows up from the ocean, scouring the cliffs, searching me out. I should stand up. I should walk back along the sheep track, back to Hauteville House so that I am not late for supper. But I cannot move.

I knew in Bièvres that I had gone too far over the precipice. The lover's embrace is never enough when it has become everything, and I lived only for those moments in the woods, those moments in the church. All the time I was with Victor and the children I thought merely of escaping.

But I couldn't leave. Even though I had once thought of leaving, I knew I had a duty to stay. I was a wife and mother. I had been a wife and mother before I met Sainte-Beuve and that was where my true loyalty lay. That was where it should lie, although I no longer really cared for that Adèle. I wanted to step out of her, the way I stepped out of a gown at the end of an exhausting evening. But I couldn't.

There was no choice. Even when I thought I had a choice, it was never simply a matter of choice.

The walk back is a blind stumble along the dirt track, my mind racing forwards and backwards. I don't notice a single step I take, and yet I don't once leave the ruts and I reach the top of our street without incident.

Because I'm walking downhill towards our house I don't need to stop for breath as is necessary on the walk up. But I do stop all the same. I stop in front of the house with the pretty flowers on the lawn. This is the house Victor bought for his mistress, Juliette Drouet. This is where she lives. These are her flowers, planted by Victor in the shape of his initials on her lawn. A big, bright VH for all the townspeople to see. And if I stand here, in front of her house and look down towards ours, I can see the rag that Victor has tied around the railing in front of his upstairs room. It is a flag for her, for his mistress, to signal that he is up in the morning. He is up and thinking of her as he sets about his work and he has lashed his underwear to the railing to let her know this.

It is not just because Guernsey is full of English people that we do not take part in society. It is because society wants no part of a man who goes into exile with his wife and his mistress. They shun us. We are not invited into their homes or to their social functions.

I don't blame Juliette Drouet. When we first landed in Jersey, she kept a respectful distance from my family at the docks. She understands discretion. She never comes to the house. I never meet her on the street, or hear a word from her. I know Victor and this means that I cannot hate Juliette. Often I actually feel great sympathy towards her. She is in exile as well, and she doesn't have any children to comfort her. All she has is Victor, and having had this myself once, I know what it means. And I do believe that I had the younger, better version of the man. She must be a very patient woman to endure all his present-day demands.

If Victor isn't working on his biography of an evening, he walks up the street to see Juliette. Sometimes he will have his evening meal there. He doesn't simply need to have his family around him at the end of a day, he needs to feel loved. And his family cannot give him enough of the love he needs so voraciously – the love he feels entitled to.

The problem with our situation is not that Victor has a mistress, or even that she has come to join us in exile. The problem with our situation is that it is seemingly endless. Napoleon III is still the Emperor of France. Victor remains in opposition to him. I don't see how anything will ever change. We will remain here together on Guernsey, in our uneasy alliance, until we all die.

Charles is lounging on the terrace when I return to the house. He has been sleeping all afternoon, my lazy, fat son. Idleness is destroying him, and a false industry is destroying François-Victor. It is ridiculous to think that he can translate the entire works of Shakespeare! My little Adèle, my poor daughter, is being consumed by spectres. She is giving her life away to ghosts.

This has to end.

"Maman," says Charles, waving in greeting from his supine position, his feet raised up on cushions. "Where did you get to?"

He should be married, my little Charlot, who is not little at all. He should be married and have a family of his own. It shouldn't matter to him where his mother was for a few hours on a beautiful day.

I say nothing for fear I will say something hurtful. I just brush past him and storm into the house.

My other children must be in their rooms. Good thing, I think grimly, and head for the staircase. I pass the mirror in the front hall and catch a glimpse of myself in the glass. My hair is loose and frayed, like rope ends that have lost their splice. There is a smudge of dirt across my cheek. My eyes startle, the wild eyes of an animal.

There you are, I think as I pass on by. There you are, Adèle, at last.

I never go up to Victor's study when he is working. If not actually forbidden, it has certainly been understood all these years I have lived with him that I am not to disturb him during working hours. His genius is delicate and could easily be ruined by interruption.

I take the stairs two at a time and am battling for breath by the time I get to the top.

This room on the third floor was already a generous space before Victor added the glass box. It already had sweeping views of the ocean and sky, but the glass box has the effect of making it seem open to the elements. It is as though Victor stands in the middle of the ether. At night the stars seen through the glass roof must be dazzling, and oh so close.

Victor writes standing up at a battered, high, wooden desk. When I get to the top of the stairs he has his back to me, and in the moments before he notices that I'm there and turns around to face me, I have a glimpse of what it is like to be Victor.

The sun through the glass roof is brilliant. It illuminates every detail of the room. There is the low-ceilinged library where my husband keeps his vast collection of books. There is the Raft of the Medusa emergency bedroom where he beds, or attempts to bed, the succession of young maids who come to work in Hauteville House. There is the glass window cut into the floor in the shape of a porthole, and the mirror positioned above it so Victor can see down into the bowels of the house, can see us walking through the rooms and going about our daily business.

It must be magnificent to be Victor. Even his very name is triumphant. And here he is, at the top of the house, at the top of the world. He has the machinery of the household below him and the infinite horizon in front of him. The ocean is so flat and blue that it seems as if he could hook a finger under an edge and pull the entire sheet of shimmering fabric towards him.

Why would he not feel that he can do anything, take anything? He stands at his desk, a conductor in front of an orchestra, moving the music of the world to his whim. I understand Victor better in this moment seeing him at work than I have ever understood him during all the years we have lived together.

I understand him better, but I still blame him.

"Adèle." He greets me with surprise. "Are you all right? Has something happened to one of the children?"

"The children are fine," I say.

He puts down his pen. His fingers are as ink-stained as Dédé's. I see the lines he has written on the page in front of him as a series of small rivers, spidering delicately across the paper.

"Well, no, they're not fine." I have recovered from the climb up the stairs, but my breath is still catching in my throat and I realize that I am nervous. I have never confronted my husband before. I'm not sure I can do it. But then I think of Charles, lazing like a fat seal on the terrace; and of François-Victor, eagerly searching out each French word for Shakespeare's plays; and most of all of Adèle, disappearing day by day into the spirit world. "But the boys are men," I say. "They have chance and choice, even on this island. It is because of Dédé that I have come to see you."

"But I am working." Victor still looks completely surprised at my presence in his study. "Could this not have waited until tonight?"

The light behind Victor outlines him, makes him look like a sculpture. I notice that he even has ink on his beard, this new white beard he has grown since we've been here on Guernsey. He thinks it suits a man in exile to have a beard.

Victor Hugo

I suddenly feel exhausted.

"I have asked for nothing," I say. "I have done my duty. When you wanted to move to Jersey, I followed you. And when you felt that you had to come to Guernsey, I followed you here. You bought this house without asking me, but I said nothing.

I say nothing about the way you decorate it, or about how you spend your time. But, I am not the only one who has done her duty to you. Little Adèle has given away her youth to this exile, to *your* exile. She is languishing here, pining after a sailor she barely knows, wasting her days doing embroidery."

"But I have given her a small garden to cultivate," says Victor. "I have asked her to help collate my pages."

"She's a young woman. That is not enough to fully occupy her. She needs to be out in society. I want to take her back to Paris."

"Impossible."

He says it so quickly that I am taken aback. "Won't you even consider what I have said?" I did not say it easily. I have never said such words to my husband, and he knows this.

"There is nothing to consider. If she leaves this island it will prove that she does not love me. She must prove her love by staying. I will not be abandoned by my family."

"Not permanently, Victor. Just for a month or two. I would take her to Paris just for a little while, and then we would return here and continue to do our duty to you."

But Victor has already turned back to his desk, to his work. He has finished with our conversation.

"She is suffering! You don't know how she has suffered, how she continues to suffer." My voice is raised and shaking from emotion. I'm glad that Victor has turned away and is no longer looking at me.

He picks up his pen. "If she really loves me," he says coldly, "why would she want to leave?"

I mentioned that Hauteville House was haunted. The former resident, a vicar, apparently ran from the house, left in fear for good because of the ghost. But we Hugos are used to apparitions and we are not worried by the footsteps and the moaning. The ghost is a woman. We have all heard her low keening outside our bedroom doors at night. When we first moved into the house she was very present, but over time she has disappeared. What I think is that our misery has overtaken hers and that she has effectively been cancelled out by our greater collective woe. I lie awake at nights and no longer hear her timid steps along the hall, or her whispery voice on the other side of my door. Instead I hear Adèle tapping on the wall in the room next to mine, trying to rouse her dead sister; or I hear Victor as he rages through the house with a red-hot poker, looking for somewhere to burn his immortal words.

We are the ghosts here now. Charles, busy developing his watery photographs in the dark cupboard under the stairs. François-Victor, frantically trying to find the right echo for each word of Shakespeare's. We exist in this place as the spirits of who we used to be when we were truly alive.

Victor relented. It didn't happen immediately. But over time, and with pressure from Charlot and Toto, he allowed me to take Dédé back to Paris each year for a month or two.

But it was too late. The melancholia inflicted by the exile was not easily shaken off. Dédé was withdrawn in Paris, preferring to hole up in our hotel room writing her endless letters to Albert Pinson than to venture out into Parisian society. She had lost the facility for mixing with people. She had lost the desire to be flirtatious and witty with strangers. She saw no point in it.

I could only do so much, and in the end it turns out that I could do nothing at all.

Pinson was posted to Halifax, Canada. In the spring following this posting I made my way to Paris, on the understanding that Dédé would be joining me within the week. She packed her trunk on Guernsey and dutifully left the island, not for Paris, but for London, where, unbeknown to anyone, she took passage on a boat bound for Halifax.

This is where she is now. We had word from her that she arrived safely and that she was reunited with her sailor. She wrote home to ask for money, saying that she had married Pinson and they were happy, and that she would remain in Halifax with him, waiting for his posting to end. Although we were very upset with this arrangement, we dutifully took out an advertisement in the local Guernsey paper announcing the marriage. She writes to me occasionally, instructing me to be happy for her. She gets angry when I express any concern for her situation.

Victor is furious. She left the island without his permission. Married or not, he wants her to return. He rages around Hauteville House, beating his chest with outrage and self-pity.

I am glad Adèle is safe from her father's fury. She is on the other side of the world. It took over a month for her to travel by ship to Halifax, and Victor, despite his vitriolic outbursts, is not willing to travel that same time and distance to bring her home. Instead, we all write letters, asking her to return. She writes letters back ignoring our requests, and relating the glories of her married life.

She is lost to us.

I now remain in Paris. I cannot bear to return to Guernsey, to Victor's fury and his cloying self-pity. I write to Adèle, but I can do nothing for her. She has moved far away from my words and my embrace. She is following her own dark star and it has pulled her out of my sphere entirely. She always was half in this world and half outside it.

I would travel to Halifax to beg her to come back, but Victor won't grant me the money for the passage.

"If she truly loved me, she would come home on her own,"

is all he will say when I ask him to let me go and fetch her.

Paris has changed very little in my absence. It would have been easier for me if nothing was as I remembered. But everywhere I go, I am reminded of little Adèle, of my former life with my young family, of Léopoldine. I cannot walk past our old apartment in the Place Royale without feeling faint at the sight of it, and I weep openly outside the little shop where I used to buy cakes for my children.

It is hard to remember that there was once an ease to my days, or that I ever enjoyed myself.

I stand in the little park opposite our old apartment. Other people walk through those rooms now. A woman in a red dress stops in front of one of the tall windows and looks down at me looking up at her. It is the strangest feeling, as though I am observing the ghost of myself. Or worse, I have become the ghost of myself, standing outside my own life.

I long for the past with a fierce hunger, and there seems nothing to feed it.

Well, perhaps there is one thing.

I will go and see Charles.

PARIS, 1860s

CHARLES

HOW DID I BECOME an old man, a man in his early sixties? I stand in front of the looking glass in my bedroom as I dress for dinner, surveying myself. I am fat and bald. My forehead is twisted into a scowl and my lips are twisted into a sneer. My hands are fleshy, their nails yellow and brittle. My eyes have lost their sheen. I am not a man anyone could love. The admiration I sometimes get from younger writers is the best I can hope for. I can entice these writers to me by revealing the secrets of my contemporaries. I am not ashamed to dine out on the good name of other writers and I would show anyone's letters to anyone else who asked. My mother once accused me of keeping secrets when I was a boy. But now, in my old age, I am the opposite. I will tell all. I am not to be trusted. My bland countenance doesn't betray my wily heart. People confide in me because I appear to be harmless, and they are usually sorry.

I look around, at the long table loaded with books and papers, at the pair of mahogany bookcases against the wall, at the curtain-less iron bed, the worn armchair by the fireplace, the two bare windows that overlook the street.

I remember my rooms at the Hôtel de Rouen, how I had one for working and one for sleeping, and how pleasing that arrangement was. It strikes me, as I stand before the looking glass, that those separate rooms were symbolic of my life then, that there was a difference between my life and work, a separation. Now it is all blended together. My life is my work. I have no other.

I used to think that age ripened us; like fruit, we would become mellow as we grew older. We would relax into a version of ourselves that was the whole accumulated truth of our existence, that was the culmination of all our joys and sorrows and intellectual ideas.

But that is not what happens. We do not ripen like a peach. We grow hard in some places, soft in others. We are inflexible where we should yield, and we give way where we should hold fast.

And I wonder if it is added misery or consolation to know that when we depart this world we take with us the whole order of familiar things that have structured our days and given us comfort. What we have cared for in life and what has bound us most securely to it will no doubt accompany us, or go before us into death.

It no longer matters much what I do, so long as I have something to do – something to do in the mornings, and somewhere to go at night.

It is fortunate that I have something quite pleasant to do in the evenings these days. I belong to a dining club that meets once a fortnight at the Magny restaurant in rue Contreescarpe-Dauphine. We are all writers who gather there, some old, some young: Gavarni, Flaubert, Turgenev, Jules and Edmond Goncourt, Gautier, Renan, Taine, Charles Edmond, Eudore Soulié, and Frédéric Baudry. George Sand comes when she is in town.

What makes the dinners memorable and enjoyable is the rule we have for the club. The rule is a simple one: we are permitted to say anything at all during the dinners, but we have made a promise to one another that whatever we say will not leave the room.

What do writers talk about when they can speak freely on any subject?

Well, they don't talk about writing.

~~~~~

This evening, Flaubert wants to talk about the different head-dresses that women wear to bed.

"I am partial to the cap," he says, "but not the net."

"The net is for a lower-class woman," says one of the Goncourts. "The whores I visit wear nets."

"I have known a lady to wear a net," says Flaubert.

"Wouldn't it be a matter of comfort?" I say.

"What do your women wear?" asks the other Goncourt.

"I must confess that I have never spent the whole night with a woman."

There is shocked silence.

"On account of my work," I add, which makes no real sense, but no one cares to challenge me on it.

We move on to the mechanics of love.

"I believe," says Taine, "that women can only be satisfied in love when they are young."

"I have found the opposite to be true," says Flaubert.

"Isn't it our duty, as men, to satisfy a woman, no matter what her age?" I say.

"This from a man who has never spent the night with a woman?" says the Goncourt with the moustache, and everyone laughs.

The Goncourt brothers, Jules and Edmond, wrote a book together, a novel called *Madame Gervaisais* which had the double misfortune to be released on the day in 1852 that Napoleon III staged his coup, and to be reviewed in the press by me.

It has not met with much success.

I am too old to be impressed with the tricks of youth. The brothers' clumsy attempts at originality seemed so banal, so unoriginal, and I said so in my review.

My critique of their writing hasn't made the Goncourts feel very warmly towards me. They often take pokes at me during these dinners at the Magny. But I am too old to be provoked into a public argument.

"And that from a man who sleeps only with whores," I say in response, and get equal applause.

The evening continues. We move to the next food course, and change topics from women's nocturnal headgear to men's seminal discharge.

"I must have a discharge every two or three weeks," says Taine, "or else I cannot concentrate properly on my work. My mind is not clear."

"You are mistaken," says Flaubert. "What a man needs is not a seminal discharge, but a nervous one."

"What do you mean?" asks Renan.

Flaubert leans back in his chair. He is in good form tonight, and discoursing on love is his favourite subject.

"What a man needs is the thrill of love. Emotion. The exquisite pleasure of squeezing a woman's hand. A stolen kiss. That is what I mean by a nervous discharge, and it is so much more meaningful than a seminal one. And so much more necessary to our well-being."

"Yes," agrees Taine, "but also so much harder to come by. Many of us have wives, old mistresses, or take our pleasure at the brothel. We cannot experience what you are talking about at any of these stations. Some of us have probably never experienced this *nervous discharge*."

All along the table, heads nod in agreement.

"So, it is not very helpful then to tell us about an experience we might never have," says Taine.

"But I have experienced this," I burst out. "I have known this kind of love."

"I say again," says the Goncourt with the moustache, "this from the man who has never spent an entire night with a woman."

"But what I am talking about," says Flaubert, "does not

depend on spending a great deal of time with a woman. In fact, one is better served if this is not the case." He looks across the table at me. "Tell me about your experience of love," he says.

The other writers look at me expectantly.

Even though much of Paris probably knows about my affair with Adèle Hugo, and all of us here have promised never to talk about these dinners outside this restaurant, I just cannot bring myself to speak of her as though she were a conquest. I know Flaubert does not require me to describe my affair that way, but inevitably, once I start talking I will start boasting and my love for Adèle will become cheapened by my recounting of it.

I also cannot bear to have the Goncourts say anything cruel to me about Adèle, so I distract the group by making myself a pair of earrings out of some cherries. I offer myself up as a clown to save Adèle's honour. You see, even though I said earlier that I will talk about anything, there is still one subject I keep secret. There is still one thing I hold sacred.

Strangely enough, later in the evening, after a great deal of wine has been consumed, the talk turns to Victor Hugo.

"He wants to be a thinker," says Flaubert, "but what strikes me about his work is the absence of thought in it."

"He's a charlatan," I say. "A fake."

"Didn't I hear you say once that he taught you about poetry?" says a Goncourt.

"Perhaps, but I can't remember anything he said, so it must not have been particularly useful." I wiggle my ears with the cherries dangling from them and get a laugh. "Did you know," I say, "that Victor's beard is so coarse it damages the razors of the barber where he gets it trimmed. And his teeth are so strong he can crack peach stones with them. He has an amazing constitution. Once I climbed with him to the top of the Notre-Dame towers and he could tell the colour of the dress Madame Nodier was wearing on the balcony of the Arsenal."

I suddenly remember that perfect evening, after years of never recalling it.

Victor had decided to write his book about the cathedral, but he hadn't quite started yet. He was full of excitement about the idea, came every evening to ascend the steep stone steps of the tower, to the parapet of Notre-Dame to watch the sun go down over Paris. He begged me to accompany him on this particular day. I remember the difficulty of the climb, and how Victor bounded easily ahead of me, not breathless at all. The view was spectacular. The dome of the Panthéon could be seen, and the green splendour of the Jardin du Luxembourg. The sunset was beautiful. We talked about the cathedral, and about literature. Victor demonstrated his eagle-like sight by picking out the blue dress of Madame Nodier on the Arsenal balcony. That was in the days when our friendship was strong and uncomplicated by my feelings for Adèle.

I look around the table at the Magny. None of these men are my friends. We are bound together by a certain prestige, by our position in the literary society of Paris. But none of these men would run through the streets to my house in the early evening, bursting with an idea they couldn't wait to share with me. The truth is that I have never again had a friend like Victor, a friend so close that it sometimes felt as though we were the same person.

"Hugo said he was fated to write that book because when you stand outside the cathedral, the towers of Notre-Dame make a perfect H," says Renan.

"Typical," says Taine, and everyone laughs.

I have waited so many years for a moment like this, a moment when Victor is openly ridiculed by his peers. And yet, now that the moment has come, it brings no satisfaction with it. I can say nothing.

If I had never loved Adèle my friendship with Victor could have continued into my old age. We could have shared so much by then! Our influence on each other's writing would be profound, our knowledge of each other's minds, unparalleled.

At the end of life, the balance sheet comes out. I can't stop myself.

I always thought that my love for Adèle eclipsed everything else, that it was the one truly worthwhile thing I have done. But, realistically, the time we actually spent together lasted a mere handful of days. What if I had put that against a nurturing friendship that spanned my entire lifetime? What would I really have chosen?

Victor holds open the door for me as I struggle up the last few steps of the cathedral tower. He hauls me out onto the parapet and the wind chases us right to the edge of the stone wall. I have to hold on to the top of the wall to keep my balance.

There is an overwhelming desire to fling myself off the parapet, and I can see how tempting a death this is, why it is the choice of so many ill-fated literary heroes. In every fall there is a moment of flight. To hurtle through the air would be, for a magnificent instant, the ultimate in freedom. I shake my head to clear the thought, push against the wall to steady myself.

And just at that moment, as though he knows what I'm thinking, Victor puts his arm around me, anchoring me securely to my place on earth. My place beside him.

"Look at that," he says.

The last of the sun brushes the roofs of the buildings below, each one lit with a lambent glow. Each one beginning in shadow and ending in fire.

"All of Paris, Charles. Just waiting to celebrate us."

I SUPPOSE I AM a better friend to women than to men. It seems to be with women that I have enjoyed my most successful friendships. And now, late in life, I have made a friendship that will probably be my last.

It is with Princess Mathilde Bonaparte, the niece of the great Emperor and cousin to the man in power at the moment, Napoleon III.

Princess Mathilde is in her middle forties, at the very centre of her life. She is short and stout, full of fury and enthusiasms. She is much as I imagine her uncle to have been, if one had known him intimately. I love nothing more than to listen to her stories of Napoleon Bonaparte, even though she never met him. At the moment of her birth he was already dying on St Helena.

No matter. Her blood is his blood, and it runs fiercely through her veins.

Princess Mathilde has a weekly salon in Paris, in her magnificent house on the rue de Courcelles. She is known to all as Notre-Dame des Arts. Flaubert attends her salon regularly, as do Taine and Renan, and many others of the Magny crowd. The Princess is a formidable supporter of all the arts, and she herself is a good painter. She does watercolour copies of many of the great oil paintings in the Louvre, and she works very hard at these. She has the same tireless energy that I recognize from Victor, and have always admired.

Her house has a bust of Napoleon in the front hallway, and

much of the fabric in the house is decorated with bees, one of the emblems from Bonaparte's coat of arms. The bee is the sovereign symbol of immortality and resurrection.

Princess Mathilde has as many lapdogs as servants, and it is impossible not to trip over them when one is walking from the front hall into the drawing room. They nip at my ankles and are constantly underfoot. I have to restrain the impulse to kick at them. Needless to say, Princess Mathilde thinks very highly of these spoiled balls of fur, and I have to pretend to admire them whenever I am at the house.

Our friendship started when I began to attend her salons. At first I was just another guest, but I would often stay later than the others, engaging the Princess in conversation about her famous uncle. I told her of my early memory of seeing Napoleon, and of how I had a special fondness for Bonapartism, and for the genius of the man. This endeared me to her, and Princess Mathilde began to seek my opinion on whom to invite to her salon. She wanted a mix of generations and relied on me to keep her informed as to who among the younger writers was of particular interest. She called me her *literary adviser*, but soon she began to seek my advice on love as well as literature.

Why do women confide in me, confess to me? Do they sense perhaps that I have something of the woman in me? It must be so. And, as our friendship progressed, I told Princess Mathilde of my secret condition. Later I regretted this, for when I eventually betrayed her, she used this information to hurt me. *I am a real woman, and you are only a half man. A friendship between us was never possible.*

But the betrayal comes later. For now, my friendship with Princess Mathilde pleases us both. I visit her at her Paris house, and she comes to dine with me in mine. Adèle, my cook, always thrills at seeing the Princess's fancy four-wheeled carriage pull up outside our humble dwelling on rue du Montparnasse.

Princess Mathilde tells me about her love for the Director of the Louvre, a man who has gold buttons on his garters, and is a Count. He is also utterly unfaithful to Princess Mathilde, which causes her much distress.

We talk mostly of her struggles with her lover, although once the Princess asked me about my heart.

"What of your loves?" she said.

"Love," I replied, "is a box I dare not open."

Am I an ambitious man? There are some, like Balzac, who would say that I am, that I insinuate myself with greatness. There is the opinion that my friendship with Victor was about the advancement of my own career. No one, no one at all, seems to remember that it was I who first made Victor famous. This galls me.

Anyway, I would say that I am not ambitious, but rather that, as is natural in life, the older I get, the more comfortable I wish to be. Having an ease of circumstance when one is at an advanced age is compensation for the burdens of ageing.

I have the ear of one of the most influential people in Paris. I have a direct line to the throne.

Do I use it to better my situation?

Of course.

I do not come from a wealthy family. When Mother died she left me the house on rue du Montparnasse, but little else. The house is really quite small. The income I make from my writing is unreliable. There is no comfort in not being able to depend on one's salary, in having to struggle constantly to be paid. I am always working with an eye to how I can earn money from what I am writing. And, as I get older, the insecurity of this weighs heavily on me.

So I lobby the Princess to lobby the Emperor to make me a Senator. If I was a Senator I would be paid the fantastic sum of 30,000 francs a year simply to attend Senate meetings. This would be enough to keep me very comfortably in my old age.

When I first propose the idea to Princess Mathilde, she suggests that I come to the country house of the Emperor at Compiègne and dine with him and Empress Eugénie. She decides it will help my cause if the Emperor meets me.

And so I go, reluctantly. I am not a man used to being presented at court. I do not have the clothes or the manner for such things. But Princess Mathilde loans me a pair of court shoes and a footman to be my valet for the weekend. We travel down together in the same carriage, and I must admit that I do like the feeling of importance the occasion generates.

I look out the window of the carriage as we drive through the impressive oak and beech forests at Compiègne. The sight of the château at the end of the path through the trees makes me catch my breath. It is really a palace. "Château" is much too humble a word for it.

"To think that could have been mine," says Princess Mathilde, noting my reaction. She was once engaged to her cousin, the Emperor. "And it would have been," she adds, "if Louis hadn't decided to marry for love."

The château is even more impressive inside. There is a ballroom with gold pillars, walls of huge windows flanking each side, and several enormous chandeliers. There is a salon decorated entirely in blue – walls and chairs and drapery. My bedroom has gilt on the ceiling and an ornate marble fireplace.

I had thought that I was the only guest of the Emperor and Empress, but Mathilde just laughs when I mention this to her.

"They entertain over a hundred people a week," she says. "There will be at least forty other guests this weekend."

I don't do well at Compiègne. My court shoes pinch. My borrowed valet rolls his eyes when I get lost trying to find my bedroom after lunch in the dining room. At dinner the first night I am seated relatively close to the Empress. For a while I concentrate on the heavy silver cutlery, but when I do look up, I notice that the Empress Eugénie has a watch pinned to her vest, and that the watch does not show the right time. In fact, it does not seem to be working at all, is stuck at four o'clock, an hour long since past. I gather my courage, clear my throat and address myself to the Empress.

"Pardon me," I say, "but I can't help noticing that your watch seems to have stopped. You might want to get it repaired."

The Empress glowers at me. "I will never get it repaired," she says.

From across the table, Mathilde is waving her fork at me. Too late, I realize she's signalling me to stop talking.

"But why?" I persist.

"Because it is my lucky watch," says the Empress.

"All the more reason to get it fixed," I say.

The Empress looks over at Mathilde. "I think you need to educate your small friend," she says.

After dinner, Mathilde pulls me aside.

"Eugénie was wearing that watch when she met Louis," she says. "She was at a garden party and realized her watch had stopped, so she asked him the time. That stopped watch changed her life. She has no desire to have it repaired."

I cannot seem to get anything right. After dinner there is the choice of dancing in the ballroom, or listening to the mechanical piano in the blue salon. I choose the piano, thinking it will be less complicated than dancing, a pastime of which I've never been particularly fond. But the mechanical piano needs to be turned by a crank to play, and the Empress, seeing me enter the room, immediately volunteers me for the job. After a few rotations I am exhausted, but can't free myself until the Empress says so. She has me cranking the piano for ages, perspiration running down my face, my arm feeling as though it is going to drop off from the terrible exertion. Afterwards my arm hurts so badly that I ask my valet to massage it. He laughs and goes out to smoke in the garden.

The next morning every man, except for me, goes hunting. Mathilde asks me to come with her and the Empress on a drive to Pierrefonds to see Eugénie's collection of armour, but I decline. I can only imagine what horrible faux pas I will commit if I spend any more time in the Empress's company.

I look for the Emperor, hoping to have a chat with him about becoming a Senator, but he has gone hunting with the male guests. I look for the library, don't find it, end up in the magnificent ballroom. But here my luck changes. There is a young lady in the ballroom, a beautiful young lady, and instead of avoiding or ignoring me, she comes up to me. She offers her hand. I take it.

"Will you take me to dinner tonight?" she says.

I can't believe my good fortune.

"Of course," I say.

"Good," she says. "I'll look for you in the reception room at eight." And she turns on her delicate heel and is gone.

I search out my valet, who is chatting to one of the parlour maids in the hallway outside my bedroom.

"Where is the nearest inn?" I ask.

"Inn?"

"Somewhere to dine tonight."

"But you're a guest here," he says. "Why would you want to go and dine elsewhere?"

Princess Mathilde finally returns from her tour of the armour. I walk out with her through the garden.

"I've met the most charming young lady," I say. "And she is enamoured of me also. She has asked me to take her to dinner tonight. Do you know of anywhere nearby where we could go?"

Mathilde touches my arm and I flinch as it is still sore from winding the mechanical piano. "You don't have much experience at court, do you, Sainte-Beuve?"

"No, I suppose I don't."

"It is customary, at Compiègne, for a young woman to ask a man to escort her to the dining room. Here," says Mathilde, squeezing my arm affectionately, "at the château."

Napoleon III believes in social reform. He has been impressed with the Industrial Revolution in England which he witnessed when he was there in exile, and so his new Paris is modelled on the new London. I preferred the old labyrinth of streets to the modern boulevards. It is harder to hide in the new Paris.

An advocate of science and technology, the Emperor seems a lot less interested in literature. My attempts at conversation with him about books at dinner the next night fall flat. He keeps asking me to speak up, then loses interest in my questions about his reading habits and turns to talk to the man on the other side of him about the quality of the dinner wine.

When the list of Senators is published, I am not on it.

Like my admittance into the Académie française, my elevation into the Senate takes two tries.

And now comes the betrayal, and the end of my friendship with Napoleon's niece.

I should not have been surprised that the members of the Senate were cronies of the Emperor. Other writers in Paris assumed that I was also of this camp. They felt that I had defected from their midst, that my liberal views had just been a pretence, that my presence in the Senate was a reflection of my true political feelings. What is more true is that I am not a political man – meaning, I am not a man who is driven by politics. I have always been devoted to literature. Devotion and drive are two different things. Someone with drive likes to lead. Someone with devotion likes to serve. Politics are always the province of those with drive and direction. Action is required to advance a political movement. I had not really given up my liberal views, I was just not defined by them.

So, when one of the Senators attacked the work of Renan in a speech, I defended my Magny dining companion. And when the ratepayers of Saint-Etienne petitioned the Senate to ban certain books from their local library, I made a speech against this. (The books submitted for banning included *Candide* by Voltaire, the works of Rousseau, and all the novels of Balzac and George Sand.)

I was accused of being an atheist. One of my fellow Senators challenged me to a duel, which, thankfully, the President of the Senate dismissed.

Next up was the Press Law, which proposed charging anyone who wished to start a newspaper 50,000 francs. Of course, I had to make a speech about the inherent freedom of the press. During this speech, some of the Senators actually walked out of the chambers.

Then there was the education bill, which proposed denying a liberal education to the young. My speech about the absurdity of this brought a delegation of students to my house with flowers. I had tea with them in the garden. It was all very pleasant.

None of my liberal Senate speeches went over well with Princess Mathilde. She regarded my words and actions as treacherous. To her mind, I had supported Bonapartism until I became a Senator and then, when I was safely ensconced in the Senate, I had renounced the politics of the man who had put me there.

She had a point.

I am in my sixties when I become a Senator. I am in my sixties, and my health has begun to fail. I am afflicted in my weakest spot, by the condition that has plagued me all my adult life

– hypospadias. My bladder has become obstructed. I have had an operation to remove a stone, but nothing has really improved since then. I am still in pain. My bladder is weak and I am forced to use a catheter. During the course of a dinner party I have to rise three or four times to relieve myself. I don't believe that I have long to live. This condition that has made my life miserable will inevitably be the death of me.

So I mind losing the friendship of Princess Mathilde very much. I mind not having a confidante. I miss the intimacy. It cannot be said that this friendship was merely one of convenience for me.

But still, this is said.

I have done enough work. I do not have books hovering inside me, waiting to be released. I have written my fill. I have had my say. Work is a continuing solace to me, but I do not feel the burning need to produce another book.

There is just one thing I would like before I die. One thing I would like above all others. I have wanted this for many years and so, when it finally does happen, it seems entirely miraculous.

HALIFAX, CANADA

DEDE

MY DARLING ALBERT,

I know you will be anxious for news of me, and so I am sending word that my ship has docked and I have taken a room at the Halifax Hotel. I have registered under the name Miss Lewly, and you will find me waiting for you any afternoon that you are free to come. I have used a *nom de plume* because I want to avoid any association with Papa. It seems that he is as popular in the New World as he is in France, and I do not wish to engage in conversation about his books. I do not wish to be known here as Victor Hugo's daughter. I long, instead, to be Albert Pinson's wife.

As your French is better than my English, I am writing to you in my language.

Your beloved Adèle

My darling Albert,

I am worried that you did not receive my last letter. I think perhaps the mail service in Halifax is not what it was in France, so I have delivered this letter myself to the garrison where I know you are stationed. The soldier in the guardhouse assured me that it would find its way into your hands, and so, knowing that you will read this, I wait eagerly for a reply. Or better still, a visit. I have taken a room in the Halifax Hotel under the name of Miss Lewly. I will wait in every afternoon for your arrival there. It will be so wonderful to see you again. I have missed you so much and simply long to be in your presence.

Your beloved Adèle

Dear Maman,

Do not worry for me, Maman. I had to leave. You know how Papa is, how he would never have let me marry Albert if I had remained on Guernsey. I could only follow the man I loved, even to this dismal town that grows colder with each passing day. There was no other choice. Please understand that I did this not to hurt you, but rather to be with my beloved. Now we can be married. Nothing will make me happier than to be Madame Pinson. Please be happy for me, Maman. I beg you.

Your Dédé

My darling Albert,

I do not understand why you haven't come. I will take this letter to the garrison, and again I will ask the soldier in the guardhouse to deliver it to you. I know you are busy with your duties, but you must have a few hours free each day. I see many soldiers around the town. I have asked after you, and several of the soldiers have reported to me that you are indeed here at the garrison, and that they have seen you. Oh, if only I could be so fortunate! It was no small undertaking to leave my family, to lie about my whereabouts, to take passage, alone, across the North Atlantic. I was frightened on the ship, but I consoled myself with thoughts of you. I would do anything for you, Albert. Will you not come and see me and let me prove my love to you?

Your impatient, beloved Adèle

Dear François-Victor,

Is it not possible to prise some more coins from Papa's talons? It is costly preparing for the wedding, and I have had to outfit myself in warmer clothes for the coming winter. It is very cold in Halifax, a cold you could not imagine. Remember that day when we were children, and we awoke to snow? It was a mere dusting on the roofs and grass, but it made us so happy. Remember, dear brother? Well here, apparently, when the snow comes it can be as high as a man's chest, and so cold that one is forced to remain indoors for weeks at a time. The wind off the sea in Guernsey is nothing compared to the bitter gales that blow in from the sea here.

Nothing of the Old World is adequate to meet the demands of the New World, including my allowance. It is one thing to have a pittance while I am living at home on Guernsey, but quite another to have to survive on it here. I know you will understand, François-Victor. Please see what you can do with Papa.

Your loving sister, Adèle

My darling Albert,

You must be very busy with your duties. Vexing as it is not to see you, I understand how frustrating it must be for you to be unable to walk the few blocks to the Halifax Hotel and take me in your arms. So I will come to you, my darling. I have found out that there is to be a dance tonight at the big house at the top of the hill. (Forgive me, Albert, for not having learned the street names yet, even though I walk out every day with that very intent.) I will come to the dance and we will be reunited. I understand. It must be me who finds you. Just as I had to journey across the ocean, I will walk the final mile or so between our two bodies. Oh, to be with you again. I can hardly wait. I will wear my best dress. It is a new

one that I had sent from Paris before I left Guernsey. You
have not seen it.

Your beloved Adèle

My darling Albert,

Why did you refuse to see me at the dance? And then,
when I lingered outside, why did you come out onto the
darkened steps and tell me to leave? Why do you lie and
say that you don't love me, and that you never asked me to
come to Halifax? In Jersey you were my beloved. How can
you change your mind? Why did you tell me that you have
changed your mind? How does one stop loving, please tell
me that? How does one stop loving?

My dress was ruined from my rush back to the hotel, from
my skirts dragging in the mud. The streets are too rough here.
They are not meant for a lady. The mud, and the cold and the
darkness — it takes all my courage to remain here. Why did
you say you wanted me to return to France? How can you
mean that?

How can you stop loving me, Albert, when I love you
more than ever?

How can you?

My dear Maman,

Oh, Maman, I wish you could have been here to see the
wedding. There was such celebrating! And such dancing! We
had the reception in one of the grand houses at the top of
the hill, just up from the garrison where Albert is posted. The
house had pillars inside and out, and a ballroom decorated
with gold curtains and plaster cherubs on the ceiling. It
was so beautiful and I was so happy. I have never known
such happiness, Maman. The only happiness that could be

greater is if you had been able to attend the wedding. How it would have pleased me to have you here. But I will content myself with knowing that you will be happy for me, that you understand the sacrifices that have to be made for true love. I know you understand that, Maman. I know you understand my happiness, and that makes me love you all the more.

Your Dédé

Dear François-Victor,

Oh, that is discouraging news, dear brother. Could you not ask him again? Surely he will relent, now that Albert and I have married? It will be expensive to set up a home here, and Albert's salary is too small for such a task. Could you not persuade Papa that this could be his wedding gift to me?

I cannot wait for you to meet my new husband, brother. You and he have so much in common. You will like each other immediately. I know that. He will become a true brother to you, and that will please me greatly.

But in the meantime, François-Victor, there is the winter to get through, and I must have money to furnish our new home. Papa is stubborn, but he will listen to you. Could you not make him listen to you?

Your loving sister, Adèle

My darling Albert,

I know what it is to be afraid. I have been afraid of Papa's rages, and his strict rules for me. On Guernsey I was allowed out only to fetch the papers, and only then if I didn't go anywhere else en route.

I have been afraid that my sister no longer hears me, that she is gone somewhere far away and I won't be able to find her again.

I have been afraid that Maman will die, that she will be worn out by Papa and by the life on that miserable island, and that she will choose to be with Léopoldine, rather than with me.

I have been afraid that I would lose you, my darling husband – because even though you are reluctant to marry me, that is what you are in my heart – my true husband. I had to follow you so I would not lose you.

I have been afraid that I would drown on the crossing to Halifax. Some nights the ship groaned and heaved so much, it was like an animal trying to throw me from its back.

What keeps the fear away is my love for you. It is my only defence against it, and some days, when the fear is everywhere, I have to fight hard to remember my love. But I always do. I always triumph. So I know that you can triumph as well, that you can stop being afraid of my love and welcome it instead. I will wait, with patience, and an open heart, for that day.

Your beloved Adèle

Dear François-Victor,

Thank you for the little bit of money. I know how difficult it must have been to wrest it from Papa. I appreciate your efforts, but I urge you to keep them up. By the time the money reaches me, I am in need of more again. Just the expense involved in keeping warm during this terrible winter is considerable.

Albert and I are finding married life very agreeable. I recommend it for you, dear brother, though I understand the impossibility of meeting anyone suitable while you remain in exile with Papa. I wish that you could return to Paris without suffering his wrath. Or better yet, that you could come and make a new life here in Halifax, near to me. You would find winter an adventure, and I have heard that summer offers equal challenges, that there are large blood-sucking insects lighting on one's flesh from May to August. I am not sure why anyone would choose to live here, but I must admit that some days the fresh air sets my blood racing, and the view from the Citadel Hill at sunset is very pleasing.

You asked, in your last letter, if I regret what I have done. If I regret leaving Guernsey. I miss you and Maman so much, and Charles, and sometimes even Papa, but I do not miss the island at all. My only regret is that I did not leave it sooner.

Your loving sister, Adèle

My darling Albert,

I can no longer afford to stay in the hotel. I have moved into a boarding house down the street. It is still very close to the garrison, and I still wait for you to come and see me. Every afternoon I will be sitting in the small front parlour near to the coal fire. Even if you knock only once at the front door, I will hear you. The landlady's name is Mrs Saunders.

Your beloved Adèle

My darling Albert,

It must be very cold out on parade. I have begun to make you a scarf. I am making it in red wool, to match your uniform. It gives me solace to be making something practical for my betrothed.

Your beloved Adèle

My darling Albert,

The scarf is finished and is waiting for you. If you do not come by to try it on, I will simply have it sent to the garrison. I have begun on some gloves to accompany it.

Your beloved Adèle

My dear Maman,

You would be very proud of me, Maman. I have kept up my needlework, and my stitches have much improved. I am working on a pillow slip for my husband, an intricate design of birds in a nest. I work on it most evenings, by the coal fire in the parlour of our house. It is much too cold now to go out at nights. The wind beats against the windows like a living being, and the cold is so cold it is like a kind of heat. When the snow lashes against my face my skin feels as though it has been scalded.

But it is cosy in our little house, and I am very happy here. You should not worry about me, Maman. I know that I am far away in one sense, but in another I am as close as ever. And you know that I will always be your Dédé

My darling Albert,

It was cruel to come to the boarding house and say those words to me. It was cruel to give me that package, which I was so excited to receive, hardly daring to breathe as I opened it, then finding inside the gifts I had sent to you. All those hours over the weak coal fire, my fingers stiff with cold, making that scarf and those gloves, that pillow slip where you have never once laid your head.

I do not understand what has changed you, why you don't feel what you once did. Perhaps you could explain it to me? Perhaps then I'd be able to understand.

I stood in the hallway, after you'd gone, the cold blast of air from the open door still lingering around me. But I felt colder than that air. I felt as cold as the dead feel. I felt dead.

I cried. But it does no good to cry. No one hears you when you cry. There must be an ear for a voice, just as there must be a saucer for a cup. This letter is at least an ear for my voice, although I am not sure I will have the courage to send it to you. There was a stack of my letters in that parcel you gave me, tied neatly together with a black ribbon. Some of the envelopes not even opened.

Why do I not deserve your love, Albert? Answer me that. What have I done that is so terrible that I cannot have your love?

Your heartbroken Adèle

My dear Papa,

I cannot simply return to France. I am a married woman now. My duties are with my husband. Please stop asking me to return.

Adèle

My darling Albert,

I will heed your request, my darling. You will see no more of Adèle. She will not follow you through the streets, or wait for you outside the fancy houses where you go to dance. She will not send you any more letters – although she will continue to write them. No, you will see no more of Adèle.

I have bought myself a cane and a top hat, a coat with tails. I am reborn as Antoine Lewly. There is such freedom when I go out in the evenings now. No one gives Antoine a second glance. I can walk the frozen streets with such liberty.

I know that you are going to Bellevue House on Spring Garden Road for a dance this Saturday night with your regiment. I know this because I heard the soldiers talking outside the garrison. Have no fear, Adèle will not show up to bother you. But Antoine will be there. He can hide in plain sight, simply by being a man. Antoine can wait for you on the steps. Antoine can saunter about outside, wandering from lighted window to lighted window to catch a glimpse of you dancing. Antoine can even venture indoors and ask one of the fine young ladies of Halifax for a dance himself.

I have never known such liberty!

I feel such happiness!

Your beloved (Adèle) Antoine

Dear François-Victor,

I am disappointed in you, dear brother. A letter has arrived without a money order. Did you forget to slip it inside?

Your loving sister, Adèle

My dear Maman,

Tonight there is a dance for Albert's regiment at Bellevue House, one of the fancy houses in Halifax. It is very exciting! We will dine early and take a carriage to the house, even though it is close enough to walk. The streets here are unfit for walking in a ball gown, or for my husband to walk in his polished boots. Sometimes the streets are so muddy and torn up that boards have to placed down over the mess, and even then there are times when the boards are actually afloat in the puddles.

Nothing will make me happier than to arrive at the dance on my husband's arm. He is so handsome in his uniform. And his manners are so good. He has such confidence in all he says! I am sure he will be given an officer ranking soon. It is not right that so fine a man be only an ensign. I know this was one of the reasons Papa was opposed to the match, but does Papa not remember the days when he was simply an unpublished poet? Why does Papa take no account of anyone's ambition but his own?

You will be pleased to know that I have found a piano to practise on. I intend to keep up with my musical studies.

There is a woman who lives nearby, a Mrs Saunders, and
she has a decent piano in her parlour that she allows me
to use every afternoon, if I wish. I want to get back to my
compositions. But one needs a quiet life in order to do any
serious composing, and I fear that my life has been too busy
of late. I would also like to write a novel. Remember when
Papa said he thought I was as strong a writer as he was? Do
you think he really meant it?

Your Dédé

My darling Albert,

You did not see me last night, did you? That man who
touched the brim of his hat to you as you were crossing the
street, that was me.

I will be at all your dances, my beloved. And now that I
am Antoine, I can also go to the taverns where you like to
drink with your fellow soldiers when you are off duty. There
is no finer calling card to the world's pleasures than the dress
of a man.

Your beloved Adèle

Dear François-Victor,

It is simply not true! I do not know what lies Mrs
Saunders is telling you, but you must not believe them. I am
married to Albert. It is true that we are not living together at
the moment, and that I am living in Mrs Saunders' boarding
house, but I did not want Maman to worry about me. She
would worry if she knew that I was in a boarding house and
not living in a house of my own. So, I suppose I did lie about
that. But the other, greater lies, you must not believe those.
I am Albert's wife, and I do not go about at night dressed as
a man. Why would I do that? Ask yourself, brother, why I

would do something like that when you have never known me to be other than I am?

Your loving sister, Adèle

My dear Papa,

I have not been lying to you. Why do you never believe me?

Adèle

Dear François-Victor,

I am sorry, but if you are not going to believe me, and if you are telling Papa and Maman that I am not being truthful about what my life is like here in Halifax, then I will have to stop writing to you. Consider this your last letter from me until all the fuss dies down. I do not want Maman to come out here in the spring and bring me home. I am a married woman. Maman and Papa no longer have any claim on my liberty.

Thank you for all you have done for me. It sorrows me to think that you do not trust me to tell you the truth. But I have faced harder things than that, and I will close my heart to you for the time being, brother, just so I can continue without too much suffering. I know you will understand. We Hugos understand suffering, do we not!

I hope your translating work goes well. Do not let Papa tell you that you are too slow. I have always appreciated your measured pace, François-Victor. You have always been a safe haven for me.

Your loving sister, Adèle

My dear Maman,

This will be my last letter for a while, Maman. You know that I love you, but I fear that if you don't trust me, and I cannot convince you to do so, then I have little to say to you for the time being.

I simply want to be with the man I love, and have there be no argument about this. I know you will understand, Maman. Once you think on it for a while, you will understand.

I hope Papa is still letting you off the island. It would be good for you to be in Paris, Maman. Your true life is there. Just as my true life is here.

I embrace you.

Your Dédé

Dear Mrs Saunders,

Please excuse my damaged English. The rent, which I am not paying, will be paying soon.

Mademoiselle Lewly

My darling Albert,

I was too bold, wasn't I? I walked right into that house after you, right into the middle of that dance. Perhaps I wanted to be caught. But I certainly did not want to be pulled from the dance floor. You almost tore my arm out of its socket; you handled me so roughly. I also did not need to be dragged from the house. I would have left of my own accord if you'd simply asked me to go. I did not need to be dragged into the Poor House cemetery and be berated by you. I was not Adèle, but Antoine, and Antoine has done nothing to receive such venom from your lips.

It does no good to threaten me with the law. What would the police do? If I can be Antoine, I could be Pierre, or Sebastien. There is no stopping me. I will make you understand that you must love me. I will not leave you alone. I cannot. You must see by now that I cannot. And there is no escape. I know where you are. If your posting is changed, I will hear of it and follow you.

My love will not be denied.

It is my destiny to be with you, as it is yours to be with me. You cannot flee your destiny. I will always be right behind you.

Your beloved Adèle

My darling Albert,

What good do you think it did to send the policeman? I did not listen to a word he said. I will not do as he requests. And now, I will simply leave Mrs Saunders' boarding house and find other lodgings. The police will not find me again.

Your beloved Adèle

Dear Mrs Saunders,

I must go. Take the dresses. I leave the dresses for the money which I should be paying you. They were once made fine by a perfect Paris dressmaker. Please be having them.

Mademoiselle Lewly

CHARLES

I AM NOT EXPECTING to ever see her again, but she comes one night after I have had my supper. The tray is still on my desk and when Adèle, my cook, comes to the door of my bedroom, I think she has come simply to take the tray away.

"She's here," she says, hissing like a snake.

"George?"

"No. *Her*." Adèle fixes me with her gaze, as though the intensity of her expression will somehow convey her meaning to me. I hear slow footsteps on the staircase outside the bedroom. Whoever is here has been let in the house already and is on her way up to see me.

"The Channel Islands," says Adèle, desperately, and just as I realize what she's trying to tell me, Madame Hugo enters my room.

She has changed. She has grown stout. Her dark hair is a weave of grey. She wears a dull-coloured shawl against the chill of the evening air.

"Adèle."

"Charles."

The other Adèle is blocking Madame Hugo's entrance into my chamber. "That will be all," I say to her, and she backs, reluctantly, out of the room. I hear her footsteps hesitate on the staircase and I walk over and deliberately shut the door behind Adèle.

I am not dressed for company, am wearing only trousers and a shirt. Not even a waistcoat, and my shirt not even tucked in.

"Adèle," I say, just wanting to hear her name out loud again.

"Charles." She extends her hand. I take it. Her skin is cool from the outdoors.

"Please, sit." I wave my hand towards the chair by the fireplace and she crosses the room and takes a seat. I perch on the edge of my desk chair. My heart is thudding so noisily in my chest that I think I may faint.

"I thought you were in exile," I say.

"Victor is in exile. And it's self-imposed. I have returned to Paris for the time being."

"You've been in Paris a while then?"

"No, not very long."

The lie makes us both uncomfortable, and just as if it were a bad smell in the room, we wait for it to pass.

I have no rights to Adèle any more. I can't act petulantly, burst out with an imagined affront, beg for her affections. I grip the arms of my chair to steady myself.

"It is as though we have died," I say, unable to stop myself.

Adèle smiles at my vehemence. "We have, Charles," she says. "Don't you feel it? We have died and this is the afterlife."

My cook brings us some wine without my asking her.

"To warm you up, madame," she says to Adèle, and then she looks pointedly at me to make sure I haven't missed the allusion.

Luckily Adèle isn't paying any attention to my cook, and I am able to banish her from my room once again.

I pour a glass of wine for Adèle and take it over to her.

"Thank you." She sips at it and looks around my room, examining my desk, the window, the pictures on the wall. My room suddenly feels terribly inadequate.

"I inherited the house from my mother," I say. "It is not something I chose for myself."

"You are busy, Charles," she says, nodding towards my desk. "You are a man of industry, not idleness. I am glad."

It was all I could do, after the affair ended. I let my work consume me, feed off my bones. I have nothing else. But writing feels entirely fraudulent in comparison to love. The moment one writes about something is the moment one ceases to understand it. To write is to control experience, and to control experience is to lose its meaning. I am not saved by my work. It is just hard proof that I have lost my way.

"There was a line I particularly liked in *Livre d'amour*." She waits only a moment before summoning it. "*Time, divine old man, fades all honours.*"

"So, you read the poems, then?"

Adèle smiles and does not answer, sips her wine.

"Why are you here?" I ask.

"I have something to ask you."

"Anything."

Adèle takes another sip of her wine. I gulp half of my glass and spill several drops on my trousers.

"But before I ask you," she says, "I have something to tell you."

She tells me the story of little Adèle's voyage to Canada.

"A month at sea, all alone! That is so courageous," I say.

"Yes, it would have been courageous if Pinson had loved her," says Adèle. "But he didn't, and so it becomes an action more allied to madness than bravery."

"How did you discover the lie?"

"Dédé's landlady wrote to François-Victor because she was worried about my daughter's sanity." Adèle takes a sip of wine and smiles. "She called herself Miss Lewly in Halifax because she was afraid people might recognize her real surname."

I cannot stop myself.

"You mean Victor is famous in Canada as well?" I grind my heels into the carpet with rage.

225

"Of course. But his fame has done nothing for his temper. Those years on Guernsey he was a tyrant. No wonder she wanted to escape."

"And now she has." I pour us some more wine.

"Yes. Walking about a city not her own, using a false name and wearing male dress." Adèle pauses for a moment. "She does this in imitation of George Sand. She greatly admires her writing. For you see, she wants to be a writer like her father. And you." She takes another sip of wine, then turns her head to the window where the wind knocks against the glass. It is autumn and the trees are flinging down their leaves, challenging winter to a duel. "She has always remembered you fondly."

I had thought of little Adèle as my spiritual child. I regretted deeply that her father saw fit to keep me from her after I had confessed to him my affair with her mother. I missed my godchild. I missed the person she might have become had I still known her, the person I might have become had I been continually graced with her sweet presence.

"I wish she had been mine," I say.

Adèle turns back towards me.

"Victor always thought she was yours," she says. "That was part of the problem. He loved her less because of that. He paid her no attention. She suffered from the lack of a father's affection. I hold him to blame for this whole escapade in Halifax."

Once this might have caused me joy, to hear of Victor's failings – but they have come at the cost of Adèle's happiness, and so it brings little comfort to know of his neglect. Instead, I wish it had been different. If I had to lose Adèle and Dédé to Victor, then life with him should have made them both profoundly happy. That would have been the only compensation for my loss.

There is a knock at the bedroom door and Adèle the cook comes in to replace the wine with coffee. She is now on her best behaviour, nods deferentially to Adèle on her way out of the room. She also seems miraculously sober, probably because she doesn't want to miss a word. I'm sure she is listening outside the door. For once I wish that she were drinking, that she would stumble downstairs and pass out at the kitchen table as usual.

"Victor is furious," says Adèle. "He wants to have her committed to an insane asylum. He says that she has inherited the family trait of madness, that she is like his brother, Eugene."

"Well, it's a good thing she doesn't come home then," I say. I had forgotten the story of the Hugos' wedding, how Victor's brother went insane, screaming out his love for Adèle as he was dragged from the church.

"Your marriage didn't start well," I say.

"Don't," says Adèle. "Please, Charles. Leave the past where it is. I can't bear to go back there. I have made mistakes. We both know what those were. It won't change anything to bring them up now."

I don't know what mistakes Adèle has made. She's never said. But it slowly dawns on me that she is referring to the fact that she ended the affair with me, that perhaps remaining with Victor was the mistake. But how was she to know he would go into exile? How was she to know the effect this would have on her youngest daughter?

With Victor there was always something. He was a volatile character, his ego charging relentlessly ahead, trailing his friends and family in its wake, obsessively writing his books, always pumped up on his own virility.

"Do you think Adèle inherited our passion?" I ask.

"The strength of it?"

"The futility of it."

Adèle lurches from her chair, her body older and slower, but still driven by the force of her emotions. She kneels on the floor in front of my chair, rests her head on my lap.

"Charles," she says, "our love was the greatest pleasure in my life."

It makes me so sad to hear her utter those words, to know that her life after me has been so joyless. I stroke her hair with my hand. It is no longer silken to the touch, but coarse, like the mane of a horse.

"But, if you added up the hours we were together," I say, "it might not even equal a single week."

"It doesn't matter."

And I suddenly see that she is right. It doesn't matter. We loved each other. It is the simplest of truths, and it is not tied to a chronology. Time would not have increased what we felt.

I pat her shoulders awkwardly. Her bones are well padded with flesh. My hand is damp with perspiration and sticks to the fabric of her dress.

"You have always been with me," I say. "I have never left you."

I suddenly think of Charlotte, of the freedom I felt when I was being her, and of how she was created within my love affair with Adèle, and now is shipwrecked there.

Adèle lifts her head from my lap, struggles to regain her composure. She pushes weakly off from me and drifts slowly back to her side of the room.

"Adèle?"

She secures the combs in her hair, smoothes the front of her dress with her hands.

"I came here to ask for your help, Charles," she says. "I came here to ask you to lend me the money to travel to Halifax and bring my daughter home."

"Of course. I will give you whatever you need. Whatever I have is yours."

"But I wasn't quick enough," says Adèle. "It seems that Dédé has already left Canada. Her landlady wrote to say that she has sailed from Halifax."

"And gone where?"

"I don't know." Adèle looks out of the window again. "She is now well and truly lost to me. But you can still help me, Charles," she says.

"How?"

"You can help me not to remember the past. The pain of what I have done is too great."

We look at each other. She is still beautiful. She is still my Adèle. I can see it in her face. It flashes up, then disappears again.

I understand everything. She thought she was making the correct moral choice in staying with Victor. She thought she was protecting her children. But now she has one daughter who is dead, and another, her favourite, who is possibly mad and lost on the other side of the ocean. Her sons are well, but their lives too have been made wretched by exile. They survive. They do not prosper.

Her husband is a fire who uses all those around him as fuel for his work.

There is no recovering from Victor.

"I entrust our love to you, Charles," says Adèle. "I need some peace. I need to forget. But I would like you to remember. For both of us."

When it is time for her to leave, I walk Adèle down the stairs to the front door. Then I walk her out onto the cobblestones. The night is cold, but she insists on going back to her hotel on foot, pushing me away when I try to accompany her.

"If my daughter can wander the rough-and-tumble streets of the New World," she says, "then surely I can negotiate the familiar avenues of Paris."

She holds out her hand. I take it one last time in my own, and hold on to it for as long as I dare.

"Goodbye, Charles."

"Goodbye, Adèle."

When she turns and walks away, I want to run after her, throw myself in front of her, tell her that I love her, that it isn't too late to leave Victor, that she could still come and live with me. We could still be happy.

But I let her go without protest. I turn and walk back into my house, close the door solidly behind me, plod slowly back upstairs to my bedroom.

The room still smells of her – perfumed soap and sweat and the mustiness of age. I sit down in the chair she was sitting in by the fireplace. The fabric is still warm from her body. I close my eyes and imagine it is her embrace.

When I open my eyes I see, on my desk, the glass of cognac that Adèle the cook has poured for me in my absence, showing a sensitivity of which I had not believed her capable. I cross the room, pick up the glass, and return to the chair by the fireplace to sip the cognac.

Outside, the night continues, the city continues. Adèle is probably halfway back to the hotel by now. I didn't have the nerve to ask her where she was staying. It is unlikely to be our old haunt, the Hôtel Saint-Paul – she would have more sense than that – but I like thinking of her there nonetheless. Perhaps she has a room high up, near the roof, with a view out over the city. There would be the lights of Paris below her, and the starlight above.

I remember making love with Adèle in the room she shared with her daughter. I remember all the times we dragged Dédé with us through the orchard in the Jardin du Luxembourg, how she played in the dust at our feet while we whispered endearments and kissed one another. She would have heard everything, absorbed everything of who we were in those moments. How could she be anything other than our child – Adèle's and mine? Her hunger for love was our hunger. We have fashioned this longing in her. We have created her despair. She is living out the torment of her mother's love for me. There will be no happiness for her, and this is what is impossible for my Adèle to bear – that she sacrificed her own happiness for her children's future and instead, their future happiness has been compromised by her sacrifice.

I never see Adèle Hugo again. She dies of heart trouble in Brussels at the end of the summer, and she is buried in the cemetery in Villequier beside her eldest daughter, Léopoldine. Only her brother accompanies her body to the grave. Victor doesn't attend his own wife's funeral, preferring to remain in exile.

I hear this via Paris gossip, not through anyone I know.

After her death I read again her letters to me. I walk to our old houses on Notre-Dame-des-Champs. I sit on a bench in the Jardin du Luxembourg, in the heat of the day, and weep into my hands. There is no consolation when the walls that hold up one's world start to give way.

This should be the end of the story, but some months after Adèle's death, George Sand comes to see me.

"Have you heard?" she says, her face flushed from the rush through the Paris streets to my house. Like all of us, she is not as slim as she used to be.

"Heard what?"

"Mademoiselle Hugo is back."

"Little Adèle?"

"She followed a soldier to Barbados and was brought back to Paris by a black woman. A former slave, nonetheless." George collapses into a chair in my drawing room. "They say Mademoiselle Hugo has gone mad. Her father has had her committed to an asylum."

THE NORTH ATLANTIC

DEDE

MY BELOVED SISTER,

I still wear black for you. Every day since you died, I have dressed in mourning clothes. Every day, for over twenty years now.

I no longer sleep. I don't think I have slept for years. I walk the streets at night when I am on land. Here, on the ship, I pace the decks, the spray in my face. The salt water stings my skin and the decks are slippery. Sometimes I am thrown against the railings by the heave of the ship. The nights have no stars.

I see you ahead of me on the slope of lawn at dusk on Notre-Dame-des-Champs. You turn and your face has the gold of the sun's glow behind it. You turn and smile, because you are waiting for me to catch you up. I struggle over the grass, my small legs pumping hard. I am always so grateful when you wait for me, and always so afraid that you will not wait long enough, that you will turn away before I reach you.

Madame Baa found me shivering on the foredeck. Is that where I was? I thought I was with you.

Madame Baa is kind to me, sister. As kind as Maman. You would like her. She took me in when everyone else shunned me, thinking me mad because I walked the streets of the hot place dressed in the heavy clothes of the cold place. But I had no money. Papa had stopped sending me an allowance. If I had no money, how could I have afforded to buy new clothes?

Madame Baa says, "Quiet, child." Sometimes, when I am writing, it seems that I am also speaking the words out loud, and this is confusing to her. She thinks I will feel better if I am quiet.

Maman is dead. Do you know this? Her heart gave out. Have you seen her? I know she was buried in the cemetery at Villequier with you. Can you reach out through the cold earth and touch her?

I agreed to go on this ship, to go with Madame Baa back to France, because I longed to see Maman. But she died just before we boarded, and I could not escape the passage. Now it will be Papa who meets me at the docks. I am afraid to see Papa. I fear he will be very angry with me. He had endless patience with you. With me, he has no patience at all.

You were so good at everything, sister. I tried to do one thing with all my heart, and I failed terribly at it.

I tried to love Albert, but he would not let me. He did not want my love. He has married someone else now, an English-woman. Albert is back in England with his new English wife. He probably never thinks of me.

Madame Baa says, "Come here, child." She says, "Don't cry." Am I crying?

I must do as she says.

Halifax was cold. Bridgetown, Barbados was hot. Albert was posted there without warning, and I followed him within the very week that he sailed.

I was not prepared for the heat, just as I had not been prepared for the Halifax winter. Bridgetown was scorching. I could feel the heat of the streets through the soles of my shoes. The bonnets I wore had to be peeled from my scalp at night.

I did not deceive myself that Albert would be pleased to

see me, and I was not wrong. But my need to see him was so great that it no longer mattered what he felt about it all. I did not care that he loathed me, that he begged me to leave him alone. I just could not. I did not do it to cause him any pain, only because I had no other choice. I was drawn to him. My destiny was his destiny.

There were orders at the garrison to keep me out. I found lodgings nearby, but had to leave those quite soon because I could not pay the rent. I had taken little from Halifax, just one trunk of clothes and papers. I was allowed to keep the trunk in a shed at the landlady's house in Bridgetown, and I returned to it daily to collect and deposit papers, and to occasionally change my clothes.

I was starving and Madame Baa took me into her small house with the metal roof and fed me a stew that tasted much better than it looked.

Madame Baa is a slave. She was stolen from her homeland, a place called Trinidad, and forced to work on the sugar plantations in Barbados. She was freed only last year, and even though I ask her continually to tell me about her time as a slave, she will only say that talking about it makes her think about it, and she'd rather not do that any more. "I am a free woman now," she says. "And I am going to Paris."

Her family are all dead. Sometimes Madame Baa says that I remind her of her daughter, but I cannot see how. I think she desires everyone to remind her of her daughter. I understand that. I know what it is to lose someone and want nothing more than to see her again, to have her turn around at the top of the garden and wait for you to catch her up.

Albert did not stay long in Barbados. He was waiting for a posting back in England, and when it came through, he sailed away, went home and married that Englishwoman. I heard no more of him. Papa sent me the marriage announcement from the paper. This was cruel of him, I suppose, but Papa is angry with me for having lied. He says he would have understood if I had just told him the truth. But what is the truth, sister?

Albert sailed for home. I was living in the shadows of Bridgetown. The white women who lived in the plantations moved to the other side of the street if they saw me approaching. They seemed afraid of me. I could see it in their eyes. Only Madame Baa felt any sympathy for my position. Only Madame Baa did not judge me.

I worry that she will be stared at in Paris. I worry that she will be just as much of a curiosity in Paris as I have been in Bridgetown.

Papa paid for our passage. Madame Baa wrote to him and offered to bring me home. "I have always wanted to see Europe," she said.

If Maman is with you, sister, will you tell her that Madame Baa has looked after me like a mother, and that I would have perished without her kindness. Will you kiss Maman for me, and tell her that I wanted so much to see her again, just once more again?

Madame Baa wants me to stop writing this letter. She says it is upsetting me to think of you, to be writing like this to you. But she does not understand. If I do not think that you are still out there, somewhere, then you will cease to exist at all. And if that happens, you will disappear from my childhood. I will never have had a sister. There will be no one ahead of me on the slope of lawn at dusk.

It is not that I believe you are alive, but I believe you are somewhere. You are somewhere just out of reach. If I keep writing to you, if I keep calling out to you, then perhaps you will wait for me to catch you up. Perhaps you will hear me.

Papa was restless with the pain of your dying. Only the sea could console him. Only the sea's embrace was strong enough for him to feel. He felt that the wrong daughter had died, and he was right. It should have been me, sister. I didn't matter as much.

Victor Hugo c. 1870

I would like to be a child again. You would be alive, and Maman would be alive. We would still be living on Notre-Dame-des-Champs, with the pond in the garden, and the roses against the windows. I remember our happiness there.

A sailor has just come by to ask if I want to go below decks. He was very polite. The sailors do not know what to make of us – two women travelling together, one black and one white – but they are nice to us. I don't feel as afraid going back to France as I did coming across the ocean to Halifax by myself, those few years ago. I don't feel afraid, even with tonight's rough passage, but I am a little afraid of seeing Papa again. He does not think that I have been on an adventure. He thinks that I have fooled myself, and that in fooling myself, I have also made a fool of him. Everything is about Papa, is it not, dear Sister? You know that he was not there to bury you, but that since then he has made a big fuss of walking part of the way to your grave on the anniversary of your death and writing poems about the experience. He has written a great many poems to you. You have been his muse, and I must admit that it has made me angry. I don't want you to be a muse. I just want you to be alive again.

A wave has just drenched the back of my dress, but I have held this book to my heart and saved the paper from spoiling.

There are only a few more nights to go and then we will be in France. What waits for me? Not you. The last time you saw me I was a child. You might not recognize me now.

Could you meet me, not Papa? Could you and Maman wait for me at the docks? Please. There is enough time to crawl out of the ground at Villequier and take a carriage to the coast.

I am almost twice as old as you now. Think of that. How strange it is that you, my older sister, are so much younger than I am.

The night is swirling around me – the waves, the voices of

the sailors, the tap of the rigging. That noise sounds like the tap of the table leg on Jersey, from the table Papa told us was really you, communicating from beyond the grave. I didn't really believe you were dead then. It seems truer now, but I pray that my voice still reaches you, sister, that these words find you. I would be lost without this hope.

It's cold here, on the deck of this ship, riding through the night sea. Maman said it was sunny when you went sailing at Villequier. She said that it was a sunny afternoon and that the boat capsized suddenly and you would not have known what was happening. There would have been no pain. You would not have had time to cry out. She said that your drowning would have been swift and merciful.

Is this really true?

Was it simply a quick confusion chased by a long silence?

Was the water cold? Did you struggle?

Were you afraid, my darling?

Were you afraid?

CHARLES

THIS STORY ENDS in winter, but I write it down in spring, and in this moment, while I write this page, the sky seals over with cloud. There is birdsong outside my window, and a breeze from the north. The weather is changing. An hour ago it was sunny. The day held the promise of heat.

There is traffic on the street below. I can hear the cough of horses' hoofs and the clatter of carts. Voices rise up to my window. Words spoken on the street reach my ears as musical notes, their meaning unravelling in the air between the ground and my bedroom.

Love doesn't fail. We do.

I never loved anyone as much as I loved Adèle Hugo. And not just because I wasn't willing, or because the opportunity didn't present itself again – but because I was never again the same man I was when I was with Adèle. We met when I was thirty. I was young, full of idealism and dreams, full of energy and desire. As I have grown older, all these things have grown older too, more tepid. I have become less of myself, not more, and so by necessity any love after Adèle would be a lesser love. When I was with Adèle, I was the best version of myself that I would ever be – although I had no way of knowing this then.

And no one was ever Adèle again for me. No one treasured every part of me, treated my body as a gift. No one surprised me at the gate. No one met me with a force of passion equal to my own.

I write this story down so I can enter it again. It is as simple as that. Writing does not recreate the moment so much as it stops it. And if the moment is stopped, one is able, finally, to get a clear look at it. One can walk around it, and examine it from all sides. When a moment is in real time it is always in flight. There is nothing to do but trail after it, or run to catch up.

Who we are is determined not just by the choices we make, how we sew events together into narrative. What gives us the true measure of ourselves is how undone we can become by a single moment.

And what that moment is.

I sit in the small city church, dressed as Charlotte, waiting for Adèle to arrive. I sit three pews from the back. She will enter through the doors at the rear of the church and I want to be close to her arrival. I am always first at the church – eagerness coupled with an innate punctuality. Sitting at the back allows me to observe the front of the church – the altar and the choir loft, the stained-glass window above the altar. Sometimes it seems to me that the church is like a ship, and that the altar is the prow of this ship – with the parishioners' faith the power that moves the vessel forward.

The wood inside the church is dark, and the light coming in through the yellows and blues of the stained glass burns amber, makes the space look honeyed and warm. This belies the fact that because it is built of stone the church is always cold and damp; stone holds moisture, stone remembers cold. There is always a certain level of discomfort when one sits in a church. The pews are hard and narrow. The smell of the damp stone is sharp, a little rancid. It is natural to look for comfort when one is experiencing its opposite, and so the honeyed light seems almost miraculous. I raise my eyes to the light spilling from the altar and it is easy to believe that it is God. I am grateful for that light. I want to bask in its rays. I want to worship its source.

An empty church is just as effective as a populated one. The building was designed for both the single pilgrim, and the devout horde. When the hall is packed, and the choir is in full flight, the surge of voices cannot help but lift the spirit. In those moments it does seem possible for man to transcend his mortal faults, to exist on a more exalted plane.

When the church is empty and I am the sole human presence, there is time to contemplate the history of the building, to think about all the worshippers who came before me. When I am alone in the church it is as if my living self is the beating heart in a cavernous stone body.

I do not know which state I prefer.

In this small church there is a side chapel for the Virgin Mary. Often there are candles burning in that chapel, and I sit in my pew at the back of the hall and watch their stutter. The church is draughty and the candles lean their small flames first one way, and then another. Fire is very agreeable. It does not mind bending to the will of air.

The child-sized stone Mary stands in the arc of flickering wax. Some Virgins are defiant, staring strongly ahead, daring one to approach. Some Virgins are humble, with bowed head and clasped hands. This one is caught between the two. She has her head lowered, but her hands raised. She will not look you in the eye, but she is summoning you to come towards her embrace. I wonder at the mood of the sculptor. Her robes have deep folds, the stone gouged in channels, like rivulets, running down the length of her body.

Mary holds a crucifix. There are red and pink roses painted on the blue background behind her. The blood of Christ, turning to flowers. If I move quickly, she sometimes seems like a real person, standing quietly in the shallow alcove of her chapel, her arms extended to welcome me. I sometimes think of her like that, as a human presence, as someone who is keeping me company while I wait for Adèle. Statues always seem to be waiting. They never seem to have arrived. There is perpetually the sense of expectation in something that is deathly still.

There is a stained-glass window above Mary. It is the picture of a life-size head of Christ. The colours are simple, an arrangement of brown, yellow, and red. Jesus stares straight out at me, and he looks a little disappointed, as though he were expecting more people. I always feel apologetic when I look up at him there in his window.

Jesus is positioned so that he gazes straight ahead. He can't see Mary in her cave. And she looks down at her chipped stone feet. She can't see him either. It would be better if they could look at each other, although I suppose their aloneness is about their relationship to God. If they were looking at each other they would be in a relationship with each other and God would be forgotten.

I often think that Adèle is the stained-glass Jesus, all-powerful with the light behind her. I am more like Mary, with bowed head and beseeching arms. In fact, my Charlotte dress resembles Mary's dress. My dress has heavy blue pleats and it arranges itself stiffly around me on the pew, as though it too were made of stone.

We are waiting, all of us – Jesus, Mary, and I – for the moment when the heavy church door lurches on its hinges and opens to reveal Adèle.

As Charlotte, I am free from my own history. I can sit in the church and not think about my uneasy alliance with faith. I do not have a past. All I have is this moment of waiting for Adèle. It is so simple and so pure. It must be what true religion feels like.

The doors to the church are oak. The hinges are medieval, black iron straps and studs. They are the doors of a fortress and seem designed to keep people out, rather than to invite them in. When Adèle lifts the latch and swings the right-hand door open, it is the weight of centuries that she shifts.

The door opens. The light behind it is the real light of this day, not the eternal light of God that sifts through the stained-glass window at the front of the church. The real light always seems harsh, makes me blink my eyes and turn away.

Conversely, when Adèle first steps into the church she is not used to the darkness and can't see anything. She often stumbles on the threshold. It takes the full moment of the door swinging shut before she is able to distinguish objects inside the building.

When I ask her what she is thinking of in the moment when she enters the church, she always says, "Nothing. I'm just trying to find you."

In our arrangement, I am the one who waits, and she is the one who seeks me out. It is partially a result of our circumstances, in that she is restricted by her marriage, so she is in control of the time we spend together – but it is more than that. Our natures are thus, I think. I am more comfortable waiting. She is more comfortable seeking. Our situation, although frustrating in terms of our being able to be together, is actually in perfect accordance with who we are.

Adèle's heels are sharp on the stone floor, like the hoofbeats of a small horse. They knock and echo as she walks up the aisle, so that by the time she gets to my pew, the church rings with the sound of her steps.

I have watched her hurry up the aisle. She has seen me sitting in the pew. When she slides in beside me, we are looking only at each other.

She is always impatient. As she manoeuvres herself into the

pew she invariably bangs her knee on the upright at the end of the bench, or her elbow on the back of the neighbouring pew. It is this I adore – her regard for her comfort and safety swept aside by her need to get to me as quickly as possible.

And what do I do as she tumbles along the bench? I sit perfectly still and wait for her to reach me. It is the most exquisite of pleasures.

Adèle's hair is out of place, and sometimes there are leaves stuck through it. Her face is red from her frantic journey. She breathes like a man after sport. When she puts out her hands to grab me, they are damp with perspiration.

"Charlotte."

I love how she says my name, as though it is the last word she will ever utter. I love how she takes my face in her hands and kisses me with such abandon.

But here I go too fast again. This is the trouble with love. It has its own momentum, skips ahead like a fast heartbeat. It is hard to slow the words down enough to properly examine the moment.

When Adèle slides into the pew beside me, I forget about the rest of the church. Everything I was thinking about, everything I was looking at, is easily replaced by the joy of being next to my beloved. The world shrinks to her body, then to her face, then to her lips. I wouldn't notice if the church was entirely full of people, or if the stained-glass Jesus was suddenly sitting on the other side of me.

When I was a boy, standing on the top of that hill to watch Napoleon review his troops, I had this same feeling. When I am pulled through the early morning by a line of words, when I move further and faster along them, so that I forget myself completely, I have this feeling again. The feeling, when Adèle takes my face in her hands and kisses me, is one of surrender. No, it is more than that. It is wanting, with every part of myself, to give myself away, to spend myself, to be, finally, empty.

~~~~~

When Adèle and I meet at the hotel, I invariably arrive first. I stand outside, preferring this to waiting in the lobby, where I will be regarded with suspicion by the proprietor.

Adèle is rarely on time. It is always harder to escape from her life than she imagines it will be. One or other of the children has hurt himself and needs her maternal attentions. The person who has been pressed into looking after the children has not shown up at the correct hour. There is a shortage of cabs and she has to walk. When she is walking she trips over a piece of wood near the gutter and twists her ankle.

Whatever keeps Adèle from arriving means that I often spend a long while loitering outside the Hôtel Saint-Paul.

I walk up and down in front of the hotel. I stand against the wall, gazing fixedly at my shoes, much as the Virgin Mary does in her alcove in the church. If Adèle is taking an especially long time, I will cross the narrow street and wait there, where I have a good view of the front of the hotel, but I am not so obviously lurking.

Adèle arrives eventually and we clutch on to each other in the street, stagger up the steps and into the lobby of the hotel. We are always desperate to get to our room and the whole business of signing the register with false names seems designed as a torture to test our resolve. It always takes an infuriatingly long time to do such a simple thing as sign our names in a book.

Of course, everyone in the hotel employ knows why we're there. No one is fooled by our pretence as man and wife. For honestly, what man and wife are so desperate to have each other in the middle of the afternoon?

None come to my mind.

These remembered afternoons in our room are a perfect

balance of the satisfactions of the flesh and the spirit and the mind. Because they are so perfect I feel inadequate describing them. There is nothing to hang on to, no sharp edges. Everything swims away from me. I cannot separate myself enough from this experience to capture it for someone else. I suppose this is what happiness is, a wholeness that cannot be pried apart. The more an experience can be fractured, perhaps, the more miserable the event.

It is a lie to say that I remember my mouth on Adèle's skin, or how she tasted, or how her body closed around my hand when I was inside her. The feelings of those moments are gone forever. They were gone the instant after they happened.

So what am I remembering?

Perhaps I am not remembering; writing is not a memorial. This is just what lives in me.

I walk through the streets of Paris. It is winter. A cold wind funnels down from the north. I have dressed inadequately. By the time I get to the asylum gate I am freezing. I should have taken a cab, I'm too old for this.

I ring the bell, stamp my feet, ring the bell again.

The attendant comes out of his hut and stands on the other side of the heavy iron gate, not bothering to open it.

We regard each other for a moment.

"I've come to see one of your inmates," I say.

"Which one?"

"Adèle Hugo."

The guard eyes me suspiciously. "It's not the usual visiting hours," he says.

I reach into my pocket for some coins, pass them through the bars of the gate. "For your trouble," I say.

The asylum is a tumble of voices. It reminds me of the Académie française. A nun leads me up a stone staircase. "Her father pays for her to have her own room," she says. "Such a generous man."

I say nothing. Little Adèle would never have been put into an asylum if her mother were still alive. This is Victor's generosity. This is how Victor takes care of his children. He is still living in the Channel Islands, but he is as powerful as ever. I am not surprised that he has thought Adèle's actions insane, that he has no sympathy for her obsession with Albert Pinson.

Love, to Victor, is insanity.

We stop before a locked door.

"I will wait outside," says the nun. "Knock on the door when you are done." She produces a large iron key from a belt around her waist and unlocks the door for me.

The room is small. There is a barred window at one end, a bed along the wall, a washbasin against the other wall. The sparse furnishings remind me of the Hôtel Saint-Paul and I have to work hard to suppress a memory of Adèle lying naked on the bed there.

Little Adèle resembles her mother. She has the same dark hair and strong features. She sits in a rocking chair by the window, her head bent over a book. She looks up when the door closes behind me.

"Adèle," I say. "I am Charles. Your godfather."

She stares at me blankly. I move towards her and she shrinks away.

"Keep to your side of the room," she says.

I do.

"Charles," I say again. "I used to come to your house. I knew you when you were a little girl. I was a friend to your mother."

At the mention of her mother, Adèle's face brightens. "Maman," she says. "What will we do today, Maman?"

"I've brought you some things." I carefully hand over a copy of *Livre d'amour*. "This is a book of my poetry. Some of the poems are about you." As Adèle takes the volume, I see, on the floor by her chair, a pile of small pieces of paper and the empty covers of another book. *Les Misérables* by Victor Hugo.

"I look forward to them," she says, quite lucidly, giving no clue as to whether she plans to read my poems or shred them.

"And I have this for you." I reach into my coat pocket and bring out the square of lace, untie the ribbon and shake out the veil. "It was your mother's. She gave it to me once. I wanted to bring it for you. I thought you should have it."

Adèle takes the wedding veil, carefully examining the lacework with her long, slender fingers. She has her mother's hands, but her concentrated gaze is entirely Victor's. How could he ever have doubted that she was his?

Adèle arranges the veil over her head, making sure there is an equal length of lace hanging down both sides of her face.

"Am I pretty?"

"Very."

My legs are tired from the walk and the climb up the asylum stairs. I have been trying to present a calm demeanour to Adèle, but I suddenly feel overwhelmed.

"May I sit?" I ask. "I have come a long way."

Adèle waves a hand towards her single bed and I perch on the edge of it. I can feel the metal frame through the thin mattress.

"Is Maman coming soon?" she asks.

I don't know what to say, so I lie. "Yes. Soon."

"And are you really Charles?"

"Yes."

Adèle closes her eyes and rocks in her chair for a moment. "Charles," she says. "Charles is coming to see me. Let's open the windows, children, so that I can hear his little footsteps on the pavement." She opens her eyes, looks straight at me.

I think of myself hurrying towards the Hugo house on Notre-Dame-des-Champs, tripping over the cobblestones in my rush to get to Adèle. And I think of her waiting, perfectly still, by the open window in the drawing room, listening for the

Adèle Hugo c. 1855

slightest scuff of my shoes on the street.

I cannot help myself. I weep into my hands.

The rocking chair stops whispering against the floor. I hear

Adèle's footsteps, then the creak of the bed frame as she sits down beside me. Her tentative hand finds mine.

"Will you take me to the orchard again?" she says. "As you did when I was a little girl?"

Her skin feels cool. I hold on to her hand like a drowning man.

"Of course," I say. "Of course."

I don't know if this is possible, but I will try. I will talk to the matron on my way out, see if I can arrange this for the next time I come to visit Adèle.

"You remember the orchard?" I ask.

"You would sit with Maman," says Adèle, "on the bench by the trees. Holding her hand, just like this. I would sit on the ground by your legs. And we were all very happy. The end."

I walk home from the asylum through the orchard in the Jardin du Luxembourg. They are changing the way they grow the fruit here. The trees are now espaliered, each one trained carefully to grow its fruit in straight lines.

An apple tree lives roughly as long as a man. The trees that Adèle and I walked through are now nearing the end of their lives. They are twisted and gnarled, their leaves gone from the winter winds, their limbs crashed to the ground. The orchard is littered with these broken branches. The limbs of the old apple trees grow straight out, eventually becoming too heavy for the trunk to bear. They have dropped off and lie beneath the trees intact. It seems more like an amputation than a natural winnowing.

The new trees, with their perfect controlled shapes, grow among the old, wild trees.

The ground is cobbled with fallen fruit. But high up in one of the trees, high up in the branches, a single winter apple still clings tightly to the bough.

AUTHOR'S NOTE

SAINTE-BEUVE died on October 13, 1869 from complications following bladder surgery. The physical condition that defined his love affair with Adèle – first identified while he was at medical school, and later written about in his diaries – helped bring about his death.

Victor Hugo died on May 22, 1885, outliving both his sons by more than a decade. Adèle Hugo remained in the Paris asylum for over forty years, dying there, at the age of eighty-five, in 1915, the last surviving child of Victor and Adèle.

With few exceptions the events in my novel mirror actual events. Where possible I have used the words of Sainte-Beuve, Adèle, and George Sand.

Of the many original and secondary sources that were used in the writing of this book, I would like to especially acknowledge Harold Nicolson's biography, *Sainte-Beuve*, and I express my gratitude to the archivists at Princeton University for allowing me access to the notes he made while at work on this book.

PICTURE CREDITS

ACKNOWLEDGEMENTS

FOR THEIR BELIEF IN THIS BOOK, and their work and help to make it better, I would like to thank my agent, Clare Alexander, and my editor, Phyllis Bruce. I am more than grateful for their wisdom, acumen, and guidance – not to mention patience – during the writing of this novel.

I would like to thank Mark Siemons at Altair Electronics for computer triage above and beyond the call.

Martine Bresson translated the letters from George Sand to Sainte-Beuve. The translations of Sainte-Beuve's poetry are my own.

Professor Julie Kane generously allowed me to read her translations of Victor Hugo's poems to his daughter, Leopoldine.

Special thanks to Frances Hanna, who was the first reader of this novel.

A portion of this novel first appeared in the journal *Queen's Quarterly* in 2008.

The title of the novel is a translation of the following quote from Rimbaud: *Il faut reinventer l'amour.*

So much of the novel, and my life, has been made possible by the following people: Mary Louise Adams, Tama Baldwin, Megan Boler, Elizabeth Christie, Craig Dale, Carol Drake, Sue Goyette, Elizabeth Greene, Anne Hardcastle, Heather Home, Cathy Humphreys, Frances Humphreys, Michelle Jaffe, Paul Kelley, Hugh LaFave, Walter Lloyd, Susan Lord, Bruce Martin, Eleanor MacDonald, Jennie McKnight, Daintry Norman, Joanne Page, Anne Peters, Mike and Suzanne Ryan, Su Rynard,

Glenn Stairs, Ray and Lori Vos.

Before we knew he was dying, my brother, Martin came with me on a research trip to Paris, for which I will always be grateful.

And lastly, I would like to thank Nancy Jo Cullen, who has reinvented love for me.